Maty's eyes

With one fingertip, he slid a wayward golden strand behind her ear.

"Did you think that maybe I'd kiss you, thrust both of us back into the past?" He leaned in closer. "Maybe I'd be so overwhelmed with lust and agree to your terms."

A little closer, his lips hovered within a whisper of hers. She wasn't moving; he was positive she held her breath as her eyes dropped to his lips.

He touched her nowhere now, but damn if it didn't take every bit of his resolve to hold himself back. She had some floral scent that he didn't recognize, but it was driving him out of his mind.

"Sam," she whispered.

"Is that what you were hoping for, Maty? A little reunion sex and a closed deal?"

* * *

Scandalous Reunion by Jules Bennett is part of the Lockwood Lightning series.

Dear Reader,

I am so excited to bring you the second installment of my Lockwood Lightning series! This is the book that really sparked the series. I absolutely am a sucker for a reunion story, so Sam and Maty have been in my head for a while now... Years, actually.

Scandalous Reunion is the perfect title because these two are really in the thick of it, and they'll only have each other to rely on...if they can get beyond all the past baggage they've been lugging around.

Oh, did I mention Sam's character was inspired by Jason Momoa? No? Well...you're welcome. I wanted a big, strong, powerful billionaire who wasn't the typical suit-and-tie guy. And while Sam might be all big and burly on the outside, he has quite the soft, vulnerable spot for Maty.

There's nothing sexier than a man who will stop at nothing to protect his woman. I do hope you enjoy Sam and Maty's journey to the happily-ever-after they both deserve.

Happy reading!

Jules

JULES BENNETT

SCANDALOUS REUNION

HARLEQUIN
DESIRE

Recycling programs
for this product may
not exist in your area.

ISBN-13: 978-1-335-20910-8

Scandalous Reunion

Harlequin Enterprises ULC
22 Adelaide St. West, 40th Floor
Toronto, Ontario M5H 4E3, Canada
www.Harlequin.com

Printed in U.S.A.

USA TODAY bestselling author **Jules Bennett** has published over sixty books and never tires of writing happy endings. Writing strong heroines and alpha heroes is Jules's favorite way to spend her workdays. Jules hosts weekly contests on her Facebook fan page and loves chatting with readers on Twitter, Facebook and via email through her website. Stay up-to-date by signing up for her newsletter at julesbennett.com.

Books by Jules Bennett

Harlequin Desire

The Rancher's Heirs

Twin Secrets
Claimed by the Rancher
Taming the Texan
A Texan for Christmas

Two Brothers

Montana Seduction
California Secrets

Lockwood Lightning

An Unexpected Scandal
Scandalous Reunion

Visit her Author Profile page at Harlequin.com, or julesbennett.com, for more titles.

You can also find Jules Bennett on Facebook, along with other Harlequin Desire authors, at Facebook.com/harlequindesireauthors!

To Michael, Ryan and Christy.
Here's to all of our past distillery tours
and to the ones we've yet to take.
No such thing as too much research!

One

Sam sipped his black coffee and glanced at the stacks of mail on his desk. After being away for three weeks, the piles weren't too bad. His assistant had sorted them between junk and urgent. Sam opted to go with the junk first to get that out of the way.

As he reached for the piece on the top, his cell vibrated on his desk. He glanced to the screen, but didn't recognize the number. He set aside the piece of junk mail and answered his phone, already looking to the next piece.

"Sam Hawkins."

"Sam, hi. It's Maty Taylor."

Maty Taylor. No two words could thrust him faster or deeper into his past than the woman who'd left him brokenhearted…a woman he hadn't spoken to in sixteen years.

Refocusing on here and now, Sam struggled to catch back up to what she was saying.

"…the attorney representing Rusty Lockwood," she went on in her professional tone as if he were a total stranger…as if their intimate bond had been severed forever when she left. "I'm calling to set up a meeting."

Sam's hand froze on the letter addressed to him as he gripped his phone with his other hand.

"Maty."

Just saying her name seemed foreign, yet still so familiar, but he had to say it. He wanted her to nix the stiff tone and talk to him like she would if she ran into him on the street.

"I'm sorry, but did you say Rusty Lockwood? A meeting?" he repeated.

"Yes. I called last week and your assistant said you were out of town, so I wanted to catch you first thing this morning before your schedule got too busy."

Wait…what? Was she for real? Just calling out of the blue on behalf of his main rival and she wasn't even starting with a "Hi, how are you?" All of this was unbelievable, not to mention disappointing. How could she have any dealings with such a bastard?

"You work for Rusty Lockwood?" he double backed to ask, as he was still confused. It was too damn early for this bomb to blow up in his face. His past and present colliding to conspire against him? Oh, hell no.

When he and Maty had parted ways, he'd been in college and she was heading off to law school, set on changing the world. And where had she landed? At the door of the most crooked man Sam had ever known.

What the hell happened to the woman he knew?

"I'm his new personal attorney," Maty answered, still using that professional, polished voice. "Which explains the nature of my call. I'd like to set up a meeting to discuss my client's generous offer to purchase your distillery."

Sam snorted and dismissed the ludicrous idea. He took a seat in his leather desk chair and opened the next piece of mail.

"Your *client* is well aware that I'm not selling now or ever, so your call and this meeting are irrelevant." He pulled open a handwritten letter and smoothed it out on his desk to read. "Is that all you needed to discuss?"

"Sam," she said, her tone going from poised to nearly pleading. "I'm only asking for five minutes."

Five minutes. He wasn't giving Lockwood five seconds. The man only wanted what he couldn't have, and Sam was tired of playing this game. Sam refused to sell his distillery, and Rusty refused to take no for an answer.

"What the hell, Maty?"

"Excuse me?" Maty gasped.

"How did you get messed up with a man like Rusty Lockwood?" he asked. "He's not a good guy."

Silence greeted him on the other end and Sam shoved the letter aside as he came to his feet, waiting to hear a defense from her side.

"My professional status or my reasoning behind my position are none of your concern," she informed him. "My main focus is getting this meeting set up."

There she went again with that tone. Sam gritted his teeth and clenched his fist at his side as he turned to stare out at the mountainside and the creek running directly behind the distillery. This place was his everything and he'd be damned if he let anyone get their hands on it…especially Lockwood, even if he wanted to do it by way of Sam's ex.

"What the hell kind of game are you playing?" he demanded.

"Game?" she repeated. "I'm not playing any game. I'm simply calling on behalf of my client. Can we meet on Wednesday at one? I'll come to you."

Sam shook his head and laughed. "I'm not meeting you, Maty, but I will give you a piece of advice. Find someone else to work for instead of that bastard."

Sam disconnected the call and slid his cell back into his pocket.

What the hell was going on and what was Maty
Taylor doing back in town and working for the devil
himself?

Sam wasn't the same love-struck eighteen-year-
old he'd been, chasing after the sexy blonde four
years his senior. He'd been naive enough to think
they'd be together forever. What a joke. She chose
law school over him, but looking back, her leaving
was the biggest and best life lesson he'd ever had.
He'd learned to guard his heart, focus on his career
and build his brand.

Sam stared at the pile of mail he still needed to
go through. The handwritten letter still sat there,
but he didn't care about that. No, his mind was on
the woman who'd contacted him out of the blue. He
knew full well that wasn't the last time Maty would
try. Rusty was a persistent bastard and Maty didn't
give up on what she set her sights on, either.

Sam looked forward to seeing her again after all
these years. He only hoped she'd prepared herself
because he was stronger, more powerful and much
more experienced than the last time she'd seen him.

"Damn it"

Maty muttered her curse, but frustration coupled
with fear and anxiety pumped through her. Sam had
the nerve to laugh at her and not even attempt to
work with her on a meeting. Is that how he con-
ducted all his business?

Even though he'd been a complete jerk, he still had that low, gravelly voice that made every nerve ending stand up. Damn him for still being sexy.

And she knew he was sexy because she had seen enough photos of him over the years, and time had most definitely been kind to him.

Sex appeal or not, he still didn't have to blow off her request like she meant nothing to him. They'd shared a past, yet he couldn't find time to meet with her?

Too damn bad. She had too much at stake to let Sam call the shots. Granted her situation wasn't his fault, but he was the only solution. If there were any other way to save her brother, Maty certainly wouldn't be contacting Sam again. But Rusty couldn't be dissuaded and his blackmail scheme was impossible to get out of so she *had* to get Sam to see her, and then she had to convince him to sell his distillery to Rusty Lockwood.

Giving up wasn't an option, so Maty would just have to go to Sam.

Rusty made it clear, in very certain terms, what her duties were as his new attorney. What she'd have to do to protect her brother.

No, she didn't like being blackmailed, but she had no choice but to do Rusty Lockwood's dirty work. Since coming to Green Valley to work for Lockwood Lightning, the world's largest moonshine distillery, she'd heard rumors of Rusty's bad reputation. He was allegedly skimming money off his employees' donations to a charity for children that he supposedly supported.

Thankfully that was not her area of law so he had other lawyers, likely crooked, handling that ordeal.

No, Rusty had other plans for her, and they were only marginally related to her law experience. He'd tracked her down specifically because of her past with Sam Hawkins.

They'd been in love once, planning a future together, until she'd decided to go to law school and he'd refused to leave Green Valley. They'd had to reevaluate everything and in the end, Maty left town without looking back.

Yet here she was again after a sixteen-year absence, and if she didn't get Sam to sell his distillery, Rusty would stop payments for the care and therapy of Maty's younger brother.

If that happened…well, it just couldn't happen. Maty had no other funds, nobody to help her, nothing to fall back on. She wasn't like Rusty or Sam, both of whom had more money than they knew what to do with. She was truly alone for the first time in her life and more vulnerable than ever.

Maty pulled in a deep breath and smoothed her hand down her black pencil dress. She didn't expect approaching Sam to be an easy task. If getting him to sell his precious distillery had been easy, Rusty wouldn't have needed to enlist her help.

She nearly laughed. He hadn't *enlisted* her help. He'd demanded it. He'd removed her from her other firm in Virginia, and he'd brought her here—going so far as to set her up in an old apartment that he knew held too many memories and making it clear her brother would have all the care he needed so long as she did his dirty work.

Rusty had to have dug deep into Sam's past to find her. She and Sam hadn't had a relationship since college—though she'd never forgotten him.

She'd been four years ahead of him, more eager to jump into the career world, while he'd still been finding his way and dealing with his mother's gambling addiction.

As serious as their relationship had been, as in love as they'd declared themselves to be, so many outside circumstances had wedged between them that eventually the last tie binding them finally snapped.

Maty swallowed the lump of emotions in her throat and forced away the memories. She wasn't that same woman anymore. There was a vast difference, a lifetime practically, between twenty-two and thirty-eight. She'd experienced heartache far beyond that of losing her first love.

Though she'd still wondered about Sam over the years. It would have been impossible to ignore the explosion he had made on the scene here in Tennessee and across the country. The youngest distiller to break one billion dollars in sales in one year and the youngest master distiller in history. She couldn't go to an upscale restaurant or even a pub back in Virginia without seeing his signature bottle behind the bar.

But here in Green Valley? Nothing. The only place you could purchase Hawkins gin, and soon to be bourbon, was at the distillery itself. Rusty Lockwood kept those hard liquor licenses tied up with his moonshine. There was no way to touch the iron-fisted mogul, or his hold on the locals, and Sam was in for one hell of a fight because Maty couldn't fail. She had everything to lose.

Blackmail was a crime, but Rusty was careful not to leave a trail. He was as crooked as they came and she was in the thick of his web now. Her only edge at this stage was the element of surprise. Clearly Sam had been stunned by her Monday morning phone call. She couldn't let the momentum stop. Not only did she need to keep Sam off his game, she had to move before her fears and her memories made her call off this whole thing.

Two

An hour after he hung up with Maty, Sam stood in his office staring at the letter that he'd started to open earlier that morning.

His eyes scanned over it, then read it once more because he was positive this was a joke. Even after dissecting each and every word, he was still just as shocked as he'd been the first time through.

He had questions—so many that he didn't even know where to start. One thing he did know, though, was that he needed to get his emotions the hell under control.

This cryptic letter couldn't have come at a worse time. He didn't believe in coincidences and he was going to get to the bottom of this.

Did Maty know about this letter? Did Rusty? Was Rusty going after him even harder now that the distillery was about to launch its first ten-year bourbon?

He still couldn't comprehend how Maty had gotten tangled up with such a shady businessman.

Hearing her voice earlier had catapulted Sam into the only time in his life where he'd thought everything seemed right. For those few years when they'd been together, he'd let himself believe in a future that he now knew didn't exist.

Granted he'd been naive and in love…but all of that was in the past. He'd certainly learned his lesson in letting people in. People had to earn his trust now and he didn't make it easy for them. But once they were in his inner circle, he did everything in his power to keep them there. Friends and trusted colleagues were invaluable.

Some people who knew his past might believe he had mommy issues, but he'd never trusted his mother, so that certainly wasn't the case.

No, his skepticism stemmed from one honey-blonde, doe-eyed beauty who looked like an innocent, but gutted his heart without any qualms or regrets.

As angry as he'd been at the time, looking back, Sam realized that had she stayed, neither of them would've been happy. They both had dreams and, unfortunately for that inexperienced, naive couple, the main component of those dreams had included successful careers before personal lives.

He'd wanted to hate her that day she left him, but even then, he'd loved her. Maybe he loved her for years afterward, but now... Well, he didn't know her. Did she look the same? Had she gotten even sexier with time? He hadn't looked her up on social media, hadn't wanted to go back in time when he'd worked so hard on moving forward.

His ex coming back into town after so long wouldn't affect him. She could say or do anything she wanted and that still wouldn't change his answer on selling Hawkins. Sam pushed thoughts of Maty aside and focused on something he could actually control. He needed to figure out how to deal with this life-altering letter that had landed on his desk.

This letter, if what it said was true, changed absolutely everything he'd ever known as the truth.

All those years he'd asked his mother about who his father was and all she'd ever said was that the man was a bastard and they were all better off without him. But there were characteristics Sam had always wondered about. His mother's skin was much darker than his own, so he had always been curious what nationality or ethnicity his father was. Sam also had broad shoulders and a large frame, nothing like his mother's petite build. And the dimple he had beneath his scruffy beard. His mother didn't have dimples.

Little things that always had him wondering.

Was he holding the truth in his hands now? As

much as he wanted that chapter of his past closed, he wasn't so sure this was the closure he wanted.

Sam swiped his phone up from his desk and shot off a text to his new acquaintance and friend Nick Campbell, telling him they needed to meet as soon as possible. Not only were Sam and Nick working to bring Rusty down, but Nick was also wrapped up in this untimely letter.

Sam had met the man only a month ago, but their lives were intertwined now.

Sam grabbed the envelope to check the stamped date. Nearly three weeks ago. This must've come just after he'd left for his trip, or maybe even the day he'd left. Who knew, but clearly his assistant had put this in the junk pile by mistake.

His door flew open and Sam jerked his attention to the interruption. Joe, his loyal assistant, had wide eyes and was shaking his head.

"I'm sorry, Sam, she—"

"Good afternoon, Sam."

Maty Taylor busted through like the whirlwind he'd always remembered. The woman had always been bold, take-charge and confident. Looks like she hadn't changed.

But she had.

Her hair had gotten longer, the curls more prominent, her curves had filled out more, and that bright blue dress did nothing to hide the flare of her hips.

Get ahold of yourself. She's working for the enemy...which makes her an enemy.

Sam came around his desk and focused on Joe. "It's fine. Thank you."

Joe glanced to Maty once more before closing the double doors and leaving the two of them. Sam stood in front of his desk, crossing his arms and casually leaning against the edge. There was nothing casual about this impromptu reunion and Maty looked too damn sexy, too damn striking.

Maybe he should've researched her so he could've prepared himself for the reunion with this walking fantasy. He'd known that she'd show up. She wouldn't settle for another phone call and risk him hanging up. The Maty he'd known was hands-on and never afraid to tackle anything.

Damn, she looked too good and had him remembering too much, too fast.

Good thing his emotional walls had been erected years ago.

Hell, he'd been so naive when they'd first been together, he hadn't even realized he needed walls. He knew now.

Rusty had chosen his latest weapon well, but Sam didn't want Maty, or anyone else, in the middle of this battle. That old bastard was going to lose and he was going to make a damn fool of himself for trying all of these low-down tactics.

"I'm not selling." Sam kept his eyes locked on

hers. "You can go back and tell your boss that my answer is the same as it was when his last attorney came to me and when you called me this morning."

Maty took a step forward in a pair of leopard print heels that had way too many fantasies popping into his head—like her on his desk wearing nothing but those shoes.

"Maybe we can find a solution where both parties are happy," she suggested, a soft smile forming over her pale pink lips.

She'd rarely worn makeup when they'd been together. Now she had her deep brown eyes outlined and something sultry was going on with those lashes.

Damn it. Glossy lips and doe eyes shouldn't have his body stirring, but they did…and those damn heels weren't helping.

If he didn't keep his focus, he would succumb to this physical attraction. How could she have such an impact on him in such a short time? He'd dated over the years; it wasn't like he was never around beautiful women.

But Maty was, well… Maty.

She'd always been different and a certain part of his life still belonged only to her.

"All parties involved?" he repeated. "This party is happy just the way things are," he informed her. "If Rusty isn't contented, that's not my problem."

Maty stared at him for another minute before her

intense stare darted away, taking in his office. He watched as she made her way to the wall of black-and-white photos he had on display. He'd made somewhat of a timeline of his journey to get where he was today. He needed that reminder each and every day he entered this office, of how hard he'd worked, what all he'd accomplished, to keep him moving forward.

Of course she stopped right at the first photo of him in front of his first home-brewed beer. It had tasted like dirty bath water, but he was damn proud of that mistake. Every failure pushed him to be a better man…including the failure standing there looking like a lethal combination of brains and beauty.

"I remember this picture," she said, throwing him a glance over her shoulder.

Sam said nothing. What was there to say? She'd taken the damn picture, of course she would remember.

Maty had been there at the beginning, through his early experiments. She knew his goal of one day owning a distillery, but at seventeen, that had been so far out of the realm of possibility, he'd never dreamed it would actually happen.

When the silence stretched, Maty turned back around and Sam exhaled. Damn it. He hadn't even realized he'd been holding his breath, but when those eyes landed on him, he became paralyzed. If he didn't get his act together, she might just mesmerize him and take full advantage of his rekindled desire.

No matter what had happened in the past, there was no denying that she was even sexier than he remembered and his body didn't give a damn what had happened to his heart in the past. The ache seemed instant. He had to get her out of here.

When the quiet apparently became too much, Maty moved to the next photo. She crossed her arms and shifted her hips in a way that had his body stirring with unwanted arousal.

"You seem happy here," she murmured, tapping one perfectly polished nail against the glass.

"I graduated top of my class when I had everything stacked against me and my family to take care of."

She flashed him a glance over her shoulder. "Your mother."

Sam nodded. No need in denying the facts. Maty had been around long enough back then to know exactly the type of woman his mother was. All that had changed since Maty left, and now that Sam had money, was his mother always wanted him to bail her out of all her wrong turns.

"You didn't come here to do the whole memory lane thing," he accused, not wanting to delve into the past with her. "But you're wasting your time with anything else."

Now she turned fully, her arms dropping to her

sides as she tipped her head. "Maybe I want to catch up," she countered. "Maybe I'm curious what you've been up to these last sixteen years."

"What I've been up to?" He laughed and opened his arms wide. "Look all around you. What you and Lockwood want to take from me is what I've been up to."

Taking his heart so long ago wasn't enough? Now she wanted his life?

Because this distillery, these employees, were absolutely everything. He'd worked too damn hard, countless hours, many sleepless nights to make Hawkins a reputable business. Even if Sam died, he wouldn't pass this legacy to Rusty. There was literally no way ol' Lockwood would get his talons on Sam's distillery.

"I'm not looking to steal anything," she volleyed back. "I'm merely here on behalf of my client who is willing to up his asking price. You haven't even heard the number and it may be worth considering."

Sam hated her professional tone. Hated that she was treating him like a regular client. Hated even more that she was tied up with that bastard. But... maybe she'd changed. Maybe she didn't have morals anymore. The girl he'd once loved had been loyal to her family, put her parents and her brother above everything.

Now, she'd drawn a line between them the moment she opted to take up with his rival. He couldn't help but wonder what events over the last sixteen years had led her to make this career decision.

"How's your family?" he asked, turning the tables on her.

Maty's face paled for a second before she tipped up her chin. "My parents were killed in a car accident two years ago. My brother is still in Virginia."

All of his anger and resentment washed away at her statement. He'd loved her family like his own, so the hurt that overcame him was partly selfish.

"Maty, I had no idea," he said, taking a step forward. "I'm sorry doesn't seem adequate, but I am."

Sam forced himself to stop before he did something stupid like reach out and touch her, in a vain attempt at consoling her. He was the one who was shocked. After all, she'd had time to process the loss. Sam had always admired Will and Monica Taylor. They were loving parents, the picture of happiness with their two children who were brilliant and destined for great things.

"So is Carter an attorney, too?"

Maty blinked and spun around to the pictures. "You've had some impressive celebrities stop through here."

When she tapped the photo of a popular country singer holding up a tumbler of gin, Sam took that as his cue to stop any talk of her brother…which made Sam want to find out even more. Maty and Carter had always been close, like best friends. The fact that she was so quick to move on with another topic raised some serious red flags. They would get back to this at a later time—Sam would make sure of it.

Maty finished her perusal of the black-and-white images and blew out a sigh as she made a slow circle of his office. "You've done really well for yourself."

"I don't need your approval."

Sam relaxed against the edge of his desk and crossed his arms as he met her stare across the room. Why did he let her affect him? He'd come a hell of a long way since they were together. He was proud of where he'd landed and where he was going.

"We seem to be getting off on the wrong foot," she stated. "Is it because of the past? Because—"

"My irritation has nothing to do with the past and everything to do with your arrogant client who thinks he can have anything he wants if he whines long enough, like a toddler. He might as well move on. There are other distilleries he could look into acquiring."

"True." Maty nodded in agreement. "But he wants yours."

Sam grunted. "And you just happen, conveniently, to be the attorney assigned to this mission."

Her eyes narrowed. Her lips pursed. What he wouldn't like to do to those lips under much different circumstances.

"Mr. Lockwood is aware of our past if that's what you're asking."

"And he hired you to do what?" Sam pushed off his desk, slowly closing the gap between them. "Did he think I'd meet with you? Maybe we'd start reminiscing like we are now?"

Maty's eyes widened as Sam reached up. With one fingertip, he slid a wayward golden strand of hair behind her ear. Just as silky as he remembered.

"Maybe I'd kiss you, plunge both of us back into the past." He leaned in closer, cursing himself for being a masochist, but he couldn't stop...or perhaps he just didn't want to. "Maybe I'd be so overwhelmed with lust that I'd agree to your terms."

A little closer, his lips hovered within a whisper of hers. She wasn't moving, he was positive she held her breath as her eyes dropped to his lips.

There it was. That same crackling tension they'd always shared. That same invisible string that pulled them together no matter how hard they fought it.

Sam touched her nowhere now, but damn if it didn't take every bit of his resolve to hold himself back. She had some floral scent that he didn't recognize, but it was driving him out of his mind.

"Sam," she whispered.

"Is that what you were hoping for, Maty? A little reunion sex and a closed deal?"

Sam grazed his lips across hers, his entire body tightened with arousal as she gasped.

Get a grip, Hawkins. You're being a jerk.

Gritting his teeth and clenching his fists at his

sides, Sam took a step back. Those wide eyes still remained locked on his, but now they were a shade darker...just like they used to be when she was fully aroused.

There she was. That girl he remembered who always gave him every bit of her passion. She never could mask her desire.

Sam cursed beneath his breath and spun on his heel to circle his desk. He needed to put some space, or something substantial, between them. They'd been in the same room for ten minutes and already he wanted to slide that zipper down and see if she still liked lacy underwear.

"Go back to Rusty and tell him even you won't get me to sell," he ordered. "And maybe find yourself a client who isn't crooked, unless you are only in this for the money."

She'd never been about money before, but time changed people. Circumstances changed people. Maybe the death of her parents had done something to that moral compass of hers.

Regardless, these were not his problems and he had a company to run and a gala to prepare for in less than two weeks. He'd been gone for the past three weeks and this was only his first day back. Getting sexually distracted by his ex wasn't the best way to kick off his work week.

Maty smoothed her hair back and pasted on a smile that gave him another punch to the gut. He had a feeling she knew exactly how potent she was. Maty wasn't stupid or naive and he had to ignore her charms or any advances.

"I'll be in touch," she promised. "You might just be given a deal you can't refuse."

As she sashayed out with those swinging hips and honey hair bouncing, that's exactly what Sam was afraid of.

Sam needed a distraction, something to get his mind off the woman who'd just blown into his office and left her mark.

He stared down at his desk, at the letter he'd read earlier. It still sat on top of the envelope. It was rare for someone to write an actual letter these days, and he still couldn't believe that the words were true so he grabbed it, taking a seat as he read.

Sam,

You don't know me and by the time you receive this, I will be gone. My name is Lori Campbell. I'm Nick Campbell's mother. I do not mean to turn your life upside down, but I can't leave this world without giving my son the truth about his paternity, and I'm afraid I need to tell you as well.

Rusty Lockwood is Nick's biological father…something he just discovered. Rusty also fathered two other children and you are one of them.

I'm sorry to tell you this way, but I know my son will need family once I'm gone. He will have no one and I pray he finds someone he can lean on during this difficult time. If you would, I'd like you to reach out to him.

I hope Rusty doesn't cause trouble. I have sent a letter to the other brother as well. I wish you all well.

Lori

He still couldn't process it.

Rusty Lockwood was his biological father? How the hell did this woman know?

Sam was well connected with Nick Campbell now. They'd been acquaintances through the industry for a while, but just in the last month Nick had approached Sam about teaming up against Rusty Lockwood and putting an end to Rusty's local monopoly over hard liquor licensing.

Nick's mother had recently passed away, but Sam never knew her, never heard her name, actually.

Had Nick known Rusty was supposedly his own father? Is that why he wanted to tackle the mogul? Did he know that Rusty was Sam's father? Was that why he'd wanted to partner up?

Sam leaned forward, resting his palms on his desk. He blew out a breath and wondered what the hell he was supposed to do with all this information, all these questions.

Did he go to Nick? Did he stay quiet?

What about his mother? She'd kept this secret his entire life. Anytime he'd asked about his father, she would always say they were both better off without him. Sam had to agree, if Rusty was indeed his father. But how in the hell had his mother gotten involved with such a man to begin with?

Another realization hit him. Did Rusty know about his sons? If he did, had he shared that secret with Maty? Is that why she was back at this time to completely throw Sam off his game?

Between Maty dropping back into his life and working for the enemy, and this cryptic letter, Sam didn't know what to believe. But, one thing was for sure, he couldn't let his guard down.

He had to find out what the hell was going on.

Three

Rusty was blackmailing Maty. That could be the only explanation.

Even though she'd left him without looking back, Sam refused to believe that sweet girl from years ago had completely lost her common sense and turned so dark and unscrupulous that she'd take a job and a salary from Sam's enemy. What was her angle? Why come back to Green Valley and suddenly team up with Rusty after all this time?

Sam had had a full day of meetings and employee reviews that had occupied his time, but now that he'd gotten home and had more time to think, a black-mail scheme was all he could come up with. Not that he wanted Rusty to be holding something over her head, but Sam hated thinking the worst.

Maty had admitted that Rusty knew of her past with Sam. No doubt he'd used that as the foundation for this game plan, but there had to be more than Maty and Sam's old connection bringing her here. What could Rusty have dangled in front of Maty?

Money? Maybe, but Sam hoped to hell she hadn't gotten that shallow.

As he stepped onto the second-story balcony off his master suite, the cell in his pocket vibrated. Sam shifted his bourbon into his left hand and pulled out his phone.

Nick's name lit up the screen and Sam hesitated for a second. He'd forgotten he'd texted Nick earlier. After that little meeting with Maty and then that damning letter, Sam was still struggling to get his head on straight.

Pulling in a deep breath, Sam swiped to answer the call.

"Hawkins."

"Sam, it's Nick. Sorry I'm just getting back to you. Silvia and I were at the site all day."

Nick Campbell and Silvia Lane had started a working relationship when Nick hired Silvia to be the lead architect on his late mother's mountainside resort. Sam didn't know the dynamics of their relationship, but he did know they were now married and expecting a baby. Everything seemed to be falling into place for Nick now, even after his world had crumbled when his mother passed. Sam had to assume she had written the letter close to her passing, knowing the end was near.

"Is something wrong?" Nick asked. "Your text seemed urgent."

Something wrong? If Rusty Lockwood was his father—*their* father—then yes, something was wrong.

"It is urgent, but I'd rather not discuss this over the phone." Sam swirled his bourbon around his ice sphere. "Are you free in the morning?"

"This sounds serious."

"It is."

"Then I'm free in the morning," Nick declared. "Should I come to your office?"

"Eight o'clock," Sam confirmed. "My assistant won't be in until nine, so we'll have some privacy."

"Should I be worried?" Nick asked.

Sam had no clue how to answer that. "I just came across some information on Rusty and since we're working together on trying to get that license overturned, I wanted to share this sensitive material with you as soon as possible."

"You've piqued my interest. I'll be there."

Sam disconnected the call and tossed back his bourbon. Yes, the amber liquid should be savored and sipped. Sam wasn't in a savor and sip mood.

He wanted hard and fast…liquor or a woman, he didn't care which.

Maty instantly came to mind.

Those curves had filled out even more since she'd been twenty-two. Her body wasn't the only thing that had changed. Her entire personality had shifted. What had once been fun and bubbly now seemed cold and closed off. She was hiding something and Sam should listen to his head and leave her be…but he couldn't. Something held her to Rusty and something, or someone, had her scared. Sam wouldn't want anyone to be in that position, let alone someone he used to care for.

Rusty was clearly using Maty because of Sam, so he couldn't just ignore the situation. Well, he could if he was a cold bastard like Lockwood, but Sam wasn't anything like that man.

The man who could possibly be his father.

Was that even true? He could go to his mother and find out, but she had always been so insistent that she never wanted to discuss his father, saying they never needed him. And she'd been too busy wasting her life at blackjack tables to really care anyway.

Sam was a big boy now—he could more than handle his own and with this letter surfacing, he couldn't just dismiss what could be hard facts.

Sam would confront his mother when he was ready. He was still trying to process everything himself and he had a feeling Nick might hold even more of the puzzle pieces Sam needed.

This alliance they'd already formed weeks ago to bring Rusty down had forged a friendship. But how would Nick react once Sam revealed the letter Lori had sent?

Maty had just taken off her boxing gloves when her phone chimed. She swiped the perspiration from her forehead with the back of her arm and reached for her cell on the window ledge.

The first thing she'd done when she'd moved into this tiny apartment was put up her heavy bag. Some people drank when they were stressed, some ate their feelings, but Maty preferred to punch and kick things. She also enjoyed art, but that was for when she had a calmer frame of mind. Her mood right now was far from calm.

She glanced at her screen and saw Rusty's name. A 7:00 a.m. call from the bane of her existence? Not how she wanted to start her day.

"This is Maty," she answered.

"Miss Taylor, I worried when I didn't hear from you yesterday," Rusty started. "How did the meeting go with Sam?"

Maty pulled in a deep breath and reached for her water bottle. "We had a good talk."

"Good as in he agreed to the terms?"

Maty forced herself to remain calm. "I warned

you going in that he wouldn't agree to anything at the first meeting. Sam loves that company that he's built and getting him to sell will take some time."

"That's something you don't have," he reminded her. "The month will be up before you know it."

As if she needed the recap of the ticking clock. Rusty not only blackmailed her into coming to Green Valley, but he'd given her a timetable that would be impossible to manage given even the best of circumstances…and these were far from great circumstances. Her stress level was at an all-time high; she worried about her mental state. But she worried more about failing her brother who needed the health care Rusty was paying for.

Maty had to jump through every hoop Rusty put in her path. She had to carry out his plans, no matter what she thought of the man or his schemes.

She had come back to Green Valley with every intention of succeeding and facing Sam Hawkins. The meeting with him actually went better than she thought. She managed to be in the room with him without apologizing for leaving so long ago, without throwing herself all over him because he was still the sexiest man she'd ever known, and he didn't claim to hate her. All in all, things could've been worse. Though she did leave with a whole host of brand new fantasies because he'd gotten broader, rougher, edgier. Everything about him exuded power—he was a man not to be messed with.

Yet here she was, doing exactly that.

Maty took a long pull of her cold water. She weighed her words to Rusty as she took a seat on the bench beneath the window.

"Yesterday was the first day," she explained. "You've had other attorneys attempt this bargain and even you yourself couldn't close the deal in several months, so don't expect a miracle on day one."

"I *expect* you to make this happen or you will not like the end result."

Intimidation seemed to be the key component Rusty used to wrap people in his plans. A man like Rusty would use any means necessary to get what he wanted. Likely that's how he'd landed where he was today.

Threats were how he'd gotten her to this point and as strong as she'd always prided herself on being, Rusty Lockwood had found her weak spot and used it to his full advantage. As if her life hadn't been degraded enough, now she had to work for the devil himself.

No doubt Sam thought she had turned into some kind of shark lawyer with only a paycheck in mind. As if she needed to give him more reasons to dislike her. Just the idea that Sam could hate her left a yawning pit in Maty's stomach. Out of all the people in the world, she truly cared what Sam thought of her.

She couldn't blame him for not wanting to sell his distillery, though. Why would he? He'd taken over a floundering company nearly a decade ago and turned it into a huge success. Within the next few years, his brand would be all over the world.

Sam had always had a very detailed dream and he was living that vision every single day. He sure as hell didn't need the money.

That was the thing about Sam that Rusty would never comprehend. Sam wasn't in this industry for the money. He was here for the passion, the process. He'd always loved creating and studying and learning from his mistakes.

Rusty was about the almighty dollar and how padded his accounts could be, and that would ultimately be his downfall.

Unfortunately, his downfall didn't seem to be coming anytime soon. And Maty had gotten herself caught in Rusty's clenches. Until she could figure out a solution to all her problems—like winning the lottery—she was stuck.

"You were supposed to use your connection to charm him," Rusty added.

Maty clenched her teeth. She wanted nothing more than to have the power and the courage to tell Rusty exactly what she thought of him and this plan. She wished like hell she had the funding to care for her brother, and then she could go back to Virginia and actually live her life.

But she was stuck and she wasn't even sure the end result would turn to her favor. Rusty could end the payments for her brother's care, even if she did get this deal signed. All of this could be for nothing… but she still couldn't give up.

"Despite what you may think of me, or of any other woman you employ, I will not use sex to get what you want." The mere thought made her blood boil and her stomach tighten. "And I haven't seen Sam in sixteen years. Any bond we had is no longer relevant."

"Then make it relevant," he demanded, his voice booming.

Maty closed her eyes and gripped her water bottle, the plastic crackling beneath her fingers. She'd known going into this whole situation that luring Sam in would be an impossible task. But with her brother's care and her own reputation and career on the line, she'd had no choice.

At the end of this nightmare, she was going to have to find a respectable job and she needed to not have a giant black mark marring her name.

"I expect to be notified after each meeting," Rusty added a second before disconnecting the call.

Maty dropped her cell on the bench beside her and took another drink. She eyed her gloves and came to her feet. She might not have proper furniture, but she had a stress reliever and right at this minute, that was the most important thing.

She had to figure out how to keep her brother in the best possible care and convince Sam to give up everything he'd worked for, and she was down to twenty-nine days.

She'd never been more terrified in her life.

Sam opened the main door to the office building and let Nick pass through.

"Thanks for coming in so early," Sam stated, locking the door and motioning toward the hallway leading to his private office. "We can talk back here."

"You've been gone three weeks and you're back a whole day and find out something about Rusty that can't be discussed over the phone." Nick laughed. "That's pretty damn impressive."

Sam's gut tightened with guilt. He hadn't been totally up front and once he exposed the letter, he worried how Nick would handle the news. Surely the death of his mother was still so fresh and raw, but Lori had stated she wanted family there for Nick once she was gone. Apparently, that family was Sam.

They stepped into Sam's office and he closed the door at his back.

"I'll get right to the point." Sam crossed to his desk and picked up the envelope. "I received a letter while I was gone. It sat here for three weeks, so I had no clue it even existed."

Nick's eyes landed on the paper, then focused back up onto Sam. "This is about Rusty?"

Sam nodded. "It's from your mother."

"My mother?" Nick's eyes widened, his brows rose. "She left me a letter, too. She said that…"

Silence stretched as Nick's attention remained on the envelope. Sam waited, giving Nick time to process or make the next move. Nick had to know now exactly what this meant for both of them.

After several yawning minutes, Nick took a step forward and reached for the sheet of paper.

"Do you care if I read it?" he asked.

Sam handed it over. He kept his eyes on Nick as he unfolded the letter and read. No expression, no sign of what he was thinking or feeling. Nick's eyes got to the bottom before he started over and read through it once more.

Nick dropped the letter to his side. "Do you believe this?" he asked.

"Should I?"

Nick raked a hand over the back of his neck and stared down at the message once more. "Yeah. You should."

That's what Sam thought he would say. While Sam didn't know Lori Campbell, he doubted the woman had any reason to lie or upend her son's life once she was gone. Sam truly believed she wanted Nick to move on and find some family, and maybe she wanted to stick it to Rusty in the end, too. He couldn't say he blamed her.

Taking a step back, Sam leaned on the edge of his desk and crossed his arms over his chest. He honestly still didn't know how to wrap his mind around all of this.

"I don't know what I'm more shocked about," he stated. "That you're my half brother or that Rusty is our father."

Nick carefully folded the paper and slid it back into the envelope. "The Rusty revelation isn't new to me anymore, but I am surprised that I actually know one of my brothers."

Sam nodded. "It's all so surprising."

Nick nodded. "My mother left me a letter, too. She claimed there were two other boys that Rusty fathered. So now I know you, but there's still one missing. If he received the letter, he hasn't come forward."

"How long have you known?" Sam asked.

"I opened my letter at my mother's graveside."

Damn. That must've been a harsh blow at the worst possible time. But Nick's mom must have wanted these boys to know about Rusty for a reason. Maybe she just wanted to leave this earth with nothing on her conscience. Maybe she didn't want her son to be without family. Sam didn't know the answer, so he had to just move forward with the information he had.

And he was going to have to go to his mother and make her face her past and tell him the truth—as if their relationship through the years wasn't strained enough. He loved her, he truly did. He just didn't like her actions or the gambling habit she couldn't kick.

Sam refocused on the situation before him and vowed to talk to his mother later.

"Did you confront Rusty?"

Nick nodded and rested a hand on the back of the leather chair across from Sam's desk. "I did. You can imagine how that bastard reacted. He wasn't sorry my mother struggled as a single woman raising his child. He didn't even seem surprised that I was his son, actually."

"Are you certain about all of this, though?" Sam asked. "I'm not dismissing what your mother said, but shouldn't we have our DNA tested?"

Nick shrugged. "I don't want to confirm anything. My mother had no reason to lie and turn my life around, plus the lives of two strangers she didn't know. Taking a test won't change the way I feel about him or how he feels about me."

Sam agreed. Lori Campbell had written deathbed confessions and no matter what the truth truly was, that wouldn't change how Sam or Nick felt about Rusty. Besides, it wasn't like the old guy would welcome them into his life with open arms no matter what a test said.

"He's hired a new attorney to get me to sell Hawkins," Sam told Nick. "Maty Taylor. My ex-girlfriend from college."

Nick shifted and sighed. "Creepy that he dug that far back into your past. So how's that going?"

"I have to assume he's using her." The more Sam thought about this whole charade, the angrier he got. "I'm nearly positive he's using her because she admitted he knew about our connection. We lost touch, but I can't imagine her turning into someone who condones anything Rusty does."

He planned on making an impromptu visit to her later today. Catching Maty off guard might be the only way to get to the bottom of this entire mess. Added to that, he wanted to see her. So what if they'd ended things long ago? Sam was human and she was damn attractive. Beneath that steely, sexy facade he'd noted a vulnerability he wanted to uncover and ultimately protect. She wouldn't like it, wouldn't want him interfering, but too damn bad. If Rusty was in fact doing anything to harm her emotionally, Sam wouldn't just interfere, he'd bust onto the scene and bring Rusty down single-handedly.

"I don't even know what to say." Nick's murmur cut into Sam's thoughts. "Mom mentioned two brothers, but I had no idea if anyone would actually seek me out or even believe what they'd read."

"If I didn't know you and know your current circumstance, I'm not sure I would've believed it," Sam admitted. "I don't doubt you trust all of this to be the truth, but I'm holding out. Not that having you for a brother wouldn't be damn cool, but I sure as hell hope that ass is not my father."

But Sam could tell by the look on Nick's face that he fully believed everything his mother had said.

Sam wanted to hold on to that sliver of hope that Lori was simply mistaken.

"So what now?" Nick asked. "Are you going to go to him?"

Sam had been thinking about that since reading the letter. "No. At least, not right now. I want to wait and see how he plays this game, and I want to know what the hell he's doing with Maty."

"You still care for her?" Nick asked, quirking a brow.

Sam went with straight honesty here. How could he not care? She was the first woman who had ever captured his heart, and maybe she'd kept a piece when she left. Going to her would open up those old wounds, but he wasn't the same man now. He could see her, still appreciate her beauty and tenacity and maintain his distance.

Right?

"I care for the girl I remember. I don't know the woman she is now, but I know that Rusty has no scruples and he'd take any advantage where he saw an opening."

Nick stepped forward and laid the envelope back on the desk next to Sam's hip.

"Do you want to keep that?" Sam asked.

Nick took a step back and shook his head. "No. She meant for you to have it and I have my own letter. I hope we can still work together to team up against Rusty."

"Now more than ever," Sam agreed.

"If you decide to confront him about the paternity issue, I'll go with you."

Sam appreciated that, but at this stage, he had no idea how to handle Rusty or this information. He'd like to have more solid proof than a letter from a deceased woman. But, on the other hand, he didn't want to know.

Above all else, he wanted Maty away from Rusty. Whatever was happening here was about to explode and he didn't want her in the cross fire.

"I should be going," Nick said with a sigh. "Are we meeting at the card game this Friday?"

About a month ago, the two of them had decided to crash the good ol' boys' poker game at the local pub, Rogue Wingman. Every Friday, Rusty and a bunch of his city council cronies meet for hours of gaming and Nick had asked Sam to join him to break into the game. The united front had startled Rusty and had gotten the attention of the council members. The moonshine king wasn't the only high roller in this area and younger, smarter crews were moving in.

Sam was sure there was some poetic justice here, seeing that it was Rusty's own sons, sons he'd supposedly abandoned, who would likely bring him down. If only they knew who the third party was and if he even knew the name Rusty Lockwood, then maybe Sam and Nick would have another ally.

"I'll be there," Sam told him. "But can we keep this letter and everything under wraps for now?"

"Ashamed of being my brother already?" Nick joked.

"That's the only part I'm ready to believe is true," Sam corrected. "I just want to figure out what move to make regarding Maty and Rusty. I have to keep the upper hand for as long as I can."

Nick nodded. "I understand. I did the same thing."

After Nick left, Sam went back to his desk and stared at the letter. His past and his future were colliding. He had to be very careful about what step he took next because he wasn't going to fall into some seduction trap and lose everything he'd worked for his entire life.

But he also wasn't stupid or naive. Seeing Maty again, even after all the time that had wedged between them, only dredged up each and every spark of desire he'd ever had for her. Only that desire was ten times stronger now. Her determination combined with those new curves drew him to her even more than he would've thought possible.

How could he keep his distance? How could he ignore the pull?

He had an enemy to fight and a business to protect and the woman he wanted more than anything might just disrupt all of his plans.

Four

Maty turned down the drive lined with evergreens, surprised there weren't armed guards or something just as over-the-top to keep out unwanted guests.

Thankfully she didn't have an obstacle to get through to get to Sam's house. It hadn't taken much effort to get his address, but she thought for sure there would be a gate at the very least.

Maty was also surprised to find he didn't have a mountaintop home. He lived down in the valley with a pond and decades-old trees all around, providing privacy...not to mention this forever-long driveway.

Finally, an opening in the trees gave way to a breathtaking three-story stone-and-log home. So

very fitting for the Smoky Mountains and the surrounding areas. Not to mention very fitting for a
man as powerful and strong as Sam. He would live
in some place that was dominating and demanded
attention.

Sturdy porch swings were suspended from each
end and two rockers sat near the front double doors.
The landscaping provided variations of greenery and
a splash of color here and there. The entire place
looked like something from a magazine and she
could only imagine the inside. She already knew
she'd be sketching this masterpiece later when she
got back home.

Home. The run-down apartment that she hated
staying in. She hated the memories from each room
and if Sam ever found out where Rusty had put her…

Well, he couldn't find out.

Rusty had given her a lease in this apartment
complex, in the exact same apartment where Sam
had once lived. Everything Rusty did was methodi-
cal and deliberate.

Nerves curled through her. Coming to Sam's
home was a bold, yet necessary move. She had to
appeal to his personal side, not so much the business side. That's how Sam had always operated in
the past, through feelings and emotions, so she had
to assume he hadn't changed that much. If he wasn't
even entertaining Rusty's very generous monetary
offers, then Sam's distillery was very personal…a

point she'd tried to make to Rusty, but her words had fallen on stubborn, deaf ears.

After she pulled her car around the circular drive, Maty parked in front of the steps leading up to the wide, welcoming porch and large mahogany doors. She'd known Sam would have a magnificent home, but she'd had no idea just how taking the risk of coming here would affect her.

She'd never been more nervous and keeping her brother safe was only part of those nerves. The other bundle belonged to Sam. After all this time, she hadn't expected to feel those stirrings of desire again. She hadn't thought it possible to still have such a strong pull to someone who had been out of her life for sixteen years.

But pulled to him she was.

What if he wasn't home? What if he slammed the door in her face? What if he hated her for the way she'd left him all those years ago? What if he hated her now for the reasons she'd come back to Green Valley?

So many questions swirled around, adding to her anxiety. There was no other option and there was no backup plan. She had to rely on herself and pull up every ounce of courage and strength she could muster because she was going to need it.

Maty grabbed her bag and her cell. Her lock screen showed a picture of her and her brother. Carter was her reason for every action lately and she had no choice but to get in between two power-houses and pray she came out unscathed—and with the means to keep her brother in the care he needed.

No matter how scared or nervous she was about confronting Sam, she had to push through. Carter depended on her.

She stepped from the car and pulled in a deep breath of warm mountain air. Late spring was abso-lutely beautiful in Green Valley and coming home did help calm her nerves, somewhat. There was something peaceful about this place…so long as she ignored her reasons for returning.

Hoisting her bag on her shoulder, Maty rounded the car's hood and came to a dead stop. Sam stood at the top of the porch steps with his arms folded over his chest, staring down at her. There was no look of surprise, almost as if he'd been expecting her.

Maty gripped the strap on her bag and forced herself to take another step, and another. Fears and insecurities had no place here.

"I hope I'm not disturbing you," she said, hold-ing his gaze.

"Depends on why you're here."

She offered what she hoped was a friendly smile as she reached the bottom of the steps. "To talk. Maybe catch up. We got started off all wrong."

"By wrong, you mean telling me that you work for a man I loathe or do you mean insulting me by believing I'll sell simply because you asked?"

Okay, so he wasn't going to make this easy. Well, neither was she. There was too much at stake and much more than she'd first thought. Now she also had to worry about what would happen to her emotions by spending so much time with Sam, digging deeper into the man's psyche to try to figure out how to get what Rusty wanted.

The more time she spent with Sam, the more her attraction grew. There was no fighting a passion that had once been so alive, so fierce. She hadn't taken that buried emotion into consideration before she'd come back to Green Valley.

Since Sam hadn't asked her to leave, Maty found another layer of courage and attempted to push aside that sexual pull. She mounted the steps and came to stand next to him. Sam shifted, allowing her more space.

"Your home is beautiful," she told him, ignoring his question. "You always did want something private and out in the middle of nowhere."

Because she couldn't stand his stare another minute, Maty glanced around the vast yard and focused on the chirping birds and the butterfly on the tip of a flower petal. The tall, majestic mountains surrounding them. More fodder for her doodles later.

"How long have you lived here?" she asked.

"I built this five years ago."

She turned her attention back to him. His broad shoulders filled out his tee a little too well and Maty was having a difficult time making small talk when she really wanted to reach out and glide her fingertips over that excellent muscle tone.

"It's a big house for one man," she told him, forcing her focus to his dark eyes.

"Is that your way of asking if I'm with someone?"

Maty laughed. "Not at all. You were just never the flashy type, so I'm curious."

Sam dropped his arms and pursed his lips. "Since you drove all the way out here, I assume you have some time."

Maty nodded. "I have nothing else to do this evening."

"Follow me."

Sam stepped past the front door and waited for her. The moment Maty crossed the threshold, her breath caught in her throat. If she'd thought the outside was impressive, that was nothing compared to the spacious living area open all the way to the back of the house.

The wall of windows across the room offered a spectacular view of another pond, half surrounded by more impressive evergreens. The living room was two stories with a balcony stretching across the top that connected one side of the house to the other. Three large iron chandeliers were suspended from the ceiling. The rich, dark flooring screamed rustic luxury.

The kitchen was back in the far right, but there

were hardly any walls. A few sturdy wood beams gave support, but the structure was open and so absolutely perfect.

"I couldn't imagine living somewhere like this," she murmured, realizing her tiny apartment could fit in this entryway alone.

Maybe that's why he'd gone all out like this. Growing up in that apartment with his mother had to have been stifling and cramped. He'd always told her that when he attained his dream of owning a distillery, he would build a grand place for them to live.

For them.

They'd shared dreams at one time. Those days were long gone and that young, dewy-eyed girl now had to face the harsh reality that dreams didn't come true for everyone.

She'd had big plans of her own not so long ago. But then the crash happened, she lost her parents, she needed to provide round-the-clock care for her brother, her savings depleted...the future she'd planned was gone.

Maty would've given up all of her dreams and her career to have her family whole again. Instead, she was on the verge of losing that career and she'd have to start over with the care for Carter.

Unless she could win over Sam.

"I wanted an open space to come home to because I grew up in an apartment with just three rooms," he told her. "I knew I needed room to move."

Just what she'd figured. She was all too familiar with that three-room apartment. That's what Rusty had leased for her. Even living there alone, she felt the walls closing in on her.

Sam turned and started toward a wide staircase. "On the second floor I have three bedrooms all with their own bathrooms because when I have friends over, I want them to have privacy."

She had to walk fast to keep up as he pointed toward the wing of rooms. They weren't just bedrooms; they were literally their own suites. All breathtaking in their own way.

Sam crossed the balcony that suspended over the living room and headed up another set of steps.

"I put the master suite, the gym and the media room all up here because I wanted my own space away from where I was hosting guests."

She wondered who all stayed here. Friends? Girlfriends?

A stab of unexpected jealousy speared her. She had no reason to be jealous. She was the one who'd walked away to begin with and it had been sixteen years. It wasn't as if she'd not dated and she knew someone like Sam wouldn't have been alone, either.

Still, she didn't like the idea of him with someone else. She'd never thought of herself as a jealous person until now.

Until now, she hadn't thought she wanted Sam

with such a fierce need, but here she was barely holding it together.

Sam opened a set of double doors and she was overwhelmed by the vast home gym setup. So much equipment, from machines to weights of all sizes and even a punching bag in the corner. After all this time, they still had some things in common. Strange, since neither of them had boxed when they were together.

She didn't get a chance to comment before he closed the doors and gestured to the next room. Maty made her way toward that opening and the moment he pushed the wide doors open and revealed the new room, she smiled. There were huge leather recliners and a black screen taking up an entire wall.

"I remember how much you love movies," she told him.

"And we couldn't ever afford to go," he replied. "Mom always gambled away any extra money. I have access to all new releases the moment they hit the theater."

Maty's heart ached for that boy she remembered. She'd known his mother had a serious addiction and that their apartment had been miniscule. But when they'd been dating, Maty hadn't paid much attention to how that had affected Sam. They rarely visited with his mother and Maty always assumed Sam was just embarrassed.

"I remember always wanting to take you to see the

latest movies," he went on. "But we couldn't afford it and I was mortified. I always found some excuse rather than tell you the truth."

She'd known. Maty had been well aware Sam couldn't afford to take her. She hadn't cared about his financial status. Her parents would've given her the money to go, but she didn't want to embarrass him further or hurt his pride. Maty had been with Sam because she truly loved him and he made her laugh, made her feel alive. She hadn't been that happy since.

"This room is amazing," she told him, forcing her thoughts to the here and now. "Is that a bar with a popcorn machine?"

"You think I wouldn't have a bar in my home?" he laughed. "I have five bars in total and the popcorn is a must for movie night."

"With extra butter," she replied.

He returned her smile. "No other way."

Something shifted, breaking that thick layer of ice he'd shoved between them. Nostalgia was the way to get to him. She hated using it, hated being vindictive and stooping to the level of Rusty's commands. For a minute, she'd forgotten about Rusty and had just enjoyed the tour of Sam's house and the memories that filled her mind. But that black cloud looming over her wouldn't go away and she couldn't lose sight of why she was truly here.

No matter how she felt about Sam, in the past

or now, she had a job to do and it wasn't ending up back in his arms...or his bed.

Sam turned and went to the end of the hall where he opened another set of doors. This time he revealed his master suite. Everything in here demanded attention, from the king-sized bed on a platform in the middle of the floor to the two walls made up entirely of windows.

Even though his home was down in the valley, the views were spectacular. The mountains surrounded him, the pond looked even more vast and spectacular from here, and the sun had just started to set, casting an orange glow into the room.

"I wanted to feel like I was out in nature," he told her. "I wanted my room to feel like there are no barriers or walls around me."

Hence the windows and the bed in the center of the room. His difficult childhood had altered him, making him into the successful man he was today. She was so damn proud of him, but she couldn't tell him. If she did, he'd break her down and demand to know why she was teaming up against him.

Sam turned to face her as she remained in the doorway. "So that's why I have this big house," he told her. "Because I can. Because I won't be confined by anything or anyone ever again. I always have to be in control of my surroundings, my life."

She completely understood everything he said, but this situation wasn't in his power to control.

Rusty overshadowed both of them and there was not much she or Sam could do about it.

Maty wanted to reach for him, to console him in case the memories from the past caused him any pain. But she knew that was just a selfish move. She wanted to reach for him because he was even sexier than when they'd been together. Part of her wanted to feel those strong arms around her, and maybe she wanted to seek comfort from him. Why couldn't they console each other? At one time, they would've done just that.

Those broad shoulders threatened every single stitch in that dark gray tee. New ink poked out of his shirtsleeve and that dark hair was even more unruly than ever. There was something wildly erotic about the sight of Sam Hawkins. If people didn't know him, they'd never guess him to be a billionaire and the owner of the most up-and-coming bourbon distillery in the world. His gin had taken off years ago and the anticipation for the first bottle of ten-year bourbon was all the buzz.

It wasn't the money that made her want him. No. She wanted him because she remembered what they'd shared at one time and she couldn't help but visualize them that way again. She might have an easier time putting up resistance if she didn't know how perfect they were together, how magical his touch was, how he was the most unselfish lover she'd ever had.

Maty couldn't help but wonder if she'd made a

mistake leaving all those years ago. She wondered if law school had been worth moving away from the man she loved. But she'd wanted to explore her dreams, just as he'd stayed behind to explore his.

"So, to answer the question you didn't come right out and ask, I'm single."

She shouldn't do a happy internal dance over that news, but she was a woman and he was sexy as hell. This bedroom alone begged for sex with that bed taking center stage. Maty easily saw them tangled in those gray sheets, never wanting to leave, and rolling toward each other in the morning hours to make love again.

"And you?"

His question pulled her gaze from the bed and onto the man. "Me? What about me?"

He took a step toward her and smirked. "I assume you're single."

"Why would you assume that?" she asked, wondering if he was going to keep walking toward her.

Yes. The answer was yes as he came to stand toe-to-toe with her.

"Because if you were mine, there's no way in hell I'd let Rusty anywhere near you." Sam leaned in just a whisper more. "And if you were mine, you sure as hell wouldn't be at the home of your ex-lover."

Maty leaned back as Sam loomed over her, looking at her like he was about a breath away from kissing her…or putting that staged bed to good use.

"But I'm not yours," she murmured.

Sam slid a fingertip across her forehead, smoothing her hair back and tucking it behind her ear. That simple touch continued down her jawline and stopped just beneath her chin. He raked his thumb across her lower lip and Maty couldn't stop herself from slipping her tongue over his rough skin. His eyes widened, his jaw clenched.

"No," he agreed. "You're not."

His hand dropped, but he didn't step back.

"So, is this part of your plan?" he asked with a smirk. "Come to my home, attempt to seduce me?"

Seduce him? Maybe he'd missed the part where he'd towered over her, making her want to touch, want to remember, want to *feel*. He'd shown her his bed and they'd lingered in this room for far longer than any other. Maybe that stroke over her face and mouth wasn't affecting him the way it was her.

But he was feeling something because he wouldn't be clenching his teeth with his nostrils flared and his lips thinned if her presence meant nothing.

"I don't have a plan," she answered honestly. "I'm here to talk to you. Nothing more."

He continued to study her as if he didn't believe a word she said. But she really had no plan. Maty had prayed something would just come to her once she arrived, and something had—a heavier dose of lust than what she'd experienced in his office.

Well, she'd wanted to connect with him on a personal level… She was getting her wish.

But lust wouldn't solve her problems. In fact, getting swept away by physical emotions and a flood of memories would cause only more issues and she already had enough.

And why wouldn't he step back and give her space?

"You wanted me to kiss you," he told her. "If I were to guess, you want more."

Maty tipped her chin and leveled his gaze. "You can guess all you want. And so what if I did think about a kiss? Maybe I—"

In a flash, Sam covered her mouth with his. Whatever she was about to say vanished with that powerful, potent kiss.

Yes, she was definitely relating to him on a personal level, but suddenly the sale of Hawkins was the last thing on her mind.

Five

Sam didn't know what the hell he was doing, but he knew he didn't want to stop.

Something in him snapped…something he'd brought all on himself. He'd taunted her, wanting her to admit why she'd come here. A big part of him didn't want her to say it, though. He didn't want to think that she would use her body to get what she wanted. That wasn't the Maty Taylor he had known. No matter what had happened since they parted ways, he'd never believe that's who she'd become.

She might have come here to talk, but she was also curious. That much was obvious from their first encounter when her eyes had raked over him.

Sam gripped her hips as he continued to devour her mouth. He nearly pulled back, until her fingers threaded through his hair and she let out one of those moans that always used to drive him out of his mind.

Damn it. Some things never changed. Even after all of this time, she still came alive in his arms. How could they pick up where they left off? How could this passion still be alive after all this time?

Sam cupped her backside and walked her a few steps to the door frame. As he lifted her against his body, she wrapped her legs around his waist and circled her arms around his neck.

"Sam," she murmured against his lips.

There was need in her tone, a need that matched his own.

But he couldn't do this. Damn it. As much as he wanted her, he couldn't take her to his bed…yet. He hadn't seen her for sixteen years and she was working for his enemy. He wasn't a young, horny eighteen-year-old who couldn't control his hormones.

Besides all of that, he had to focus on his business and trying to get his mother back on track. He didn't have time for distractions even if they came in the form of his sexy ex-lover.

Reluctantly, Sam released her to slide down his body and find her footing. Maty blinked and licked her lips.

"What are you doing?" she whispered.

"Saving both of us from a mistake."

And damn if it wasn't costing him his sanity right now. He thought he'd throw her plan back in her face, but all he did was get his body all revved up with nowhere to go.

"You kissed me."

As if he needed the reminder of who started this charade. He should've stayed on his porch and talked with her. Maybe he should've just asked her to turn around and head right back down his driveway.

But no. He'd had to show off and then get all cocky and bring her to his bedroom.

"Are you telling me that when you came to my house you didn't think that's what would happen? Because I'll call you a liar if you say yes."

Maty tucked her hair behind her ears and smoothed it all over one shoulder as she took a step toward him.

"Maybe I did think of kissing you," she replied. "I'm not sorry we kissed. I enjoyed it, actually, until you stopped."

Always so bold, so demanding. He'd loved that about her when he'd been younger, now...well, he would reserve his opinion for a later time, but an assertive woman was never a turnoff.

He was a masochist. He knew it as well as anything, but that knowledge didn't prevent him from curling his fingers around her hip and jerking her forward.

"So you're saying had I not stopped, you would've let things progress?" he asked.

Her eyes glossed over with another layer of arousal. "Why not? Clearly we're still attracted to each other."

His other hand went to the snap on her jeans.

Stop this madness before someone gets hurt.

But the devil on the other shoulder urged him on and Sam had always been a risk taker. He wouldn't be where he was today had he not stepped outside his comfort zone.

"We're different people than we used to be." The button slid through the opening and he eased her zipper down, watching her eyes for any indication he should stop. "I'm not naive like before."

"You weren't naive." Her breath came out on a sigh when his knuckles scraped against her bare skin just above her panties. "We were in love."

Love? They hadn't even known what that term meant, though they'd tossed it around at the time.

All that was happening now was pure lust because he had a need for her, a need to see her come undone, to know that he was in charge and giving her exactly what she needed.

Perhaps that was a little of his past bruised ego coming to the surface, but he didn't care. Maty jerked her hips, silently urging him on as she continued to hold his gaze.

The damn woman was daring him and he never, ever turned down a dare.

Sam braced one hand beside her head and slid his other into her panties. Her gasp must've surprised her because she cut it off with a sexy bite to her bottom lip.

Gritting his teeth, he eased one finger into her. She groaned as her body arched. Sam continued to pleasure her, all the while taking in each and every facial expression and sweet little moan.

Her pale fingers curled around his dark wrist and that was just about the sexiest sight to see—her completely unashamed of taking what she wanted.

Sam worked her until she cried out and gripped his shoulders. He didn't want the moment to end, he wanted to draw out her pleasure so he could remember every aspect once she was gone and he was left in this big house all alone.

When her body ceased trembling, Sam eased his hand away and straightened her clothes. For the record, she did apparently still enjoy lace. Ironically, so did he.

Maty's head had dropped back against the door frame and her eyes remained shut tight. The silence seemed to be deafening now and he had to take a step away, to put some distance between them before he continued what he'd started.

He shouldn't have done that, but he wasn't sorry he did. Maty had always been so passionate, so responsive, and right now he was a selfish bastard. They weren't the same lovers they had been…no, this grown up version of Maty was so much more in every way. She hadn't even tried to hold back; she'd let that pleasure roll over her and he only hoped she didn't have regrets.

"You still want to talk?" he finally said when the silence stretched too long.

Her lids fluttered until those expressive brown eyes met his. "Talk," she repeated, licking her lips.

She straightened from the wall and offered a soft smile. "You want to go from that to talking? You really have changed."

Sam crossed his arms, not because he didn't want to dive back into her, but because he did. Diving headfirst into a mistake might feel good for a while, but the end result wouldn't change this situation. She was still the enemy as far as he was concerned. A sexy, sultry enemy.

"I haven't changed," he countered. "I see something I want and I go after it."

She quirked a brow. "And you wanted to give me an orgasm with nothing in return?"

"Is that so hard to believe?"

Maty tipped her head, narrowed her eyes and studied him. "I've never met a man like you."

Sam weighed that statement, jealousy spearing him when he had no room for such nonsense. She'd been with other people, just as he had, but that didn't mean he wanted the visual thrown in his face when he still felt her coming undone around him.

"You'll never meet a man like me," he countered.

"So now what?" she asked, smoothing her shirt down over her pants. "Do we go back to the tour? Christen another room?"

Sam couldn't help but laugh at her bold questions and he figured she was only half joking. Shoving his hands in his pockets, he shrugged.

"You came to me," he told her. "What do you want? The truth this time."

Maty sighed and pursed her lips. "Honestly, I want to know what you've been up to since we split. I mean, I know you're clearly a megamogul now and pretty much a celebrity, but I don't know about the personal side."

So she wanted to know more, most likely to use against him later or to take back to Rusty. Fine, Sam would play along, but he was also keeping his guard up. Something was going on with her and he had a sickening feeling Rusty was up to no good where Maty was concerned. Sam was more worried about her than he was himself. He could handle Rusty, but Maty…she had a vulnerability about her, one he didn't recall from the woman he used to know.

Besides that, Maty didn't know what an evil man Rusty was and Sam didn't want her to find out. He wanted her as far away from Rusty as possible, but she didn't seem in any hurry to remove herself from this mess.

"Follow me," he told her. "We'll take a walk around the pond. It's a nice night."

"Afraid to talk near the bed?" she joked.

Sam took a step toward her until she backed against the door frame again. He braced his hands on either side of her head and leaned in.

"Maty, when I decide to have you, I won't give a damn if there's a bed or not."

Her eyes widened with arousal and Sam pushed away, heading back downstairs before he completely lost his mind and showed her just how much he wanted her.

How long should a body keep tingling after a fierce orgasm? Because Maty wasn't sure when she'd settle, and having Sam right next to her wasn't helping matters. Neither was the veiled promise he'd made.

When I decide to have you...

Oh, he'd delivered those words with such conviction and confidence. She knew the more time she spent with Sam the more she'd feel that underlying attraction, but she'd had no clue he'd be so damn infuriating. She'd been ready to rip his clothes off and he'd brought her outside for a leisurely stroll around one of his ponds.

"I take it Virginia didn't work out for you?"

As if that's what she wanted to talk about?

"I'd rather talk about you."

The sun was still hanging on, but within the next half hour, the orange glow would be gone, replaced by a beautiful starry sky. The peaceful night surrounded by such beauty should be calming... Maty was anything but calm.

She didn't know what to say, what to feel or how to act, between the intense moment in his room, the tour where he'd basically justified why he lived in such a vast home, and the sole purpose for her being back in Green Valley to begin with. How the hell could she ever be calm again?

Maty kept in step with Sam, but he came to a stop and jerked his cell from his pocket. He cursed and shoved the phone back in, but not before Maty saw the name on the screen.

Carla Hawkins.

"You can take that," Maty told him.

"I'll call her back." The words came out through gritted teeth. "You wanted to catch up."

He started walking again and blew out a sigh. Maty didn't know the dynamics of his relationship with his mother, but she didn't want to come between them. She knew how protective Sam was toward Carla and how he'd always wanted to get help for her, but she'd refused over and over.

"How is your mom?" she asked.

"She's addicted to gambling, same as before."

His tone left no room for comment. "So why are you back? All to work for Lockwood?"

Maty slid her hands into her pockets and watched her pointed flats crush the blades of grass. "I'm back to start a new life here."

"And that new life includes working for a cold-hearted bastard?"

"I can work with any client I choose without justifying it to you or anyone else."

Sam stopped and gripped her elbow. "For someone so confident, you seem rather defensive."

She stared back at him, trying to ignore that strong, warm grip and the tingles it produced. "Fine. You want to know all about Rusty. It's simple. He wants your business."

Sam nodded. "I'm aware."

"And I'm not going to stop until I seal this deal."

Sam stared at her. His lips quirked in what seemed to be a smile, but then it vanished. "Then this should be interesting, because I would literally die protecting my company from the clutches of Lockwood."

Maty knew he meant every single word, but so did she. There had to be a way. She just had to find it.

"I know you're working overtime trying to find a way to get into my world now," he told her, dropping his hand. He took a step closer. "I'll let you in, Maty. But I won't give you a thing that belongs to me. Not my business and sure as hell not my heart."

Six

The next morning Sam still cursed himself for exposing his thoughts. He'd wanted to let Maty know, again, she was wasting her time, but somehow that young gullible man he'd once been crept up and took over all his actions.

Unfortunately, he didn't have the headspace to worry about his own issues at the moment—he had to deal with his mother's…yet again. She'd called this morning in a panic over her bills and Sam couldn't deal with hysteria over the phone, so he made the quick ten-minute drive from his home to the small mountainside cottage he'd purchased for her several years ago. He might have bought the house, but he wasn't paying her bills. He wasn't.

Sometimes he had to get tough with her because she relied on him way too much. Not that he didn't want to help, but he wanted her to help herself. That was the only way she'd get a grip on reality and stop throwing her money away.

He loved his mother, but she had a problem, and he wasn't going to be her enabler. Tough love was difficult at times because he never wanted her to think he didn't care. If he didn't care, he would leave her alone and not help at all.

And since she'd called, now was the perfect opportunity to confront her about the letter and the truth that had been revealed to him. He wanted to hear her side, to give her a chance to explain how in the hell she'd gotten tangled up with a man like Rusty to begin with.

Sam pulled into the drive behind her little red car. He grabbed his cell and stepped from his truck. His mother was on the porch swing smoking a cigarette and holding a cup of coffee in her other hand.

"Honey, you didn't have to come out here," she called to him as he started up the drive. "I'll get this figured out."

"That's what you always say." He mounted the steps and shoved his cell in his pocket. If she hadn't wanted him to come, she wouldn't have called. "How much do you owe?"

"Which person?" she asked, tears forming in her

deep brown eyes. Even with her dark skin, circles beneath her eyes showed just how stressed she was.

She always got upset over her debts, but they weren't a surprise to her, so why did she continue this vicious cycle?

"The electric company, your loan shark. Take your pick."

Her wrinkled lips thinned and she narrowed her eyes. "You're always so judgmental. Is that why you came out here? To put me down again and remind me that you have no problems?"

He had no problems? She had no clue…but she was about to get one once he sorted out this mess. His mother was usually loving and kind and compassionate, but when she got in a bind, she turned angry and mean. She was on a path of destruction that seemed to be getting worse.

"How much, Mom?"

"Including the bills that are overdue, I need twelve thousand dollars."

Twelve thousand was nothing to him, but it was a lot when discussing a damn utility payment. And it was a hell of a lot when he'd just bailed her out of another debt last week.

He wanted nothing more than for her to be trustworthy and competent. He wanted his own mother to come work for him at a dynasty he'd created, but… that wasn't reality. That fact niggled at him every single day. He wanted her by his side, he wanted them to have a trustworthy relationship, but he had to trust her first. And, for that to happen, she had to want to get better.

"That's a hell of a late fee," he replied.

"I might owe my friend Sally a few thousand," she murmured around her cigarette. "And the rest is for some bills that I didn't mention last week because I thought I could handle it."

Story of their lives. She always thought she could "handle it" and never once had that been the case.

"If Sally was your friend, she'd quit loaning you money to gamble away. And bills always come first. Always."

His mother blew out a puff of smoke and stared out at the mountains. "It's hard," she cried, the tears spilling now. "I try, Sam, you know I do. I had such a good run the other day."

Just like every day for years before that. Sam knew her routine. Wake up, fire up the coffee pot, get online to start her day of losing money. He saw the image in his mind that made up nearly every single moment of his childhood. But lately she'd seriously gotten much worse than she had been and it was time to make this madness stop.

What would it take for her to stop? What would it take for her to realize she would never recoup what she'd lost and that she needed money to live on? Where would she be if he didn't have the funds to bail her out?

She'd told him the money he received when he'd turned eighteen was from her winnings, but now he knew the truth...or what was likely the truth. Receiving money from Rusty Lockwood to keep him out of any parenting responsibilities was no doubt how Sam had received his funds.

Funds he'd used to start up Hawkins. He still didn't know how he felt about that. There was some irony in the fact that the very man who wanted to buy Sam's distillery was the one who'd funded the start-up.

"Give me the name of the woman you owe. I need more to go on than Sally, and give me your utility statements. I'll take care of them and you're not getting a penny more."

"I'm your mother." She jerked that teary gaze back to him. "I don't bring in as much money as you."

"If you took the money from your job and didn't gamble it away, you would have a nice nest egg."

She likely didn't even know what a nest egg *was*, considering she gambled away more than she made at her position as an office assistant. The simple idea of saving probably had never even crossed her mind.

This all had to stop. He'd discuss taking over her banking account, but first there were more pressing matters to dig into.

Sam crossed to the rocker and took a seat as he

watched his mother volley between her coffee and her cigarette.

He wasn't sure how to approach this subject. Sam had no clue how she'd react or if she'd even admit who his biological father was. But he'd never been one to dodge difficult subjects and this one was the biggest bomb that had ever dropped into his life. He deserved to know the truth. He also believed his mother deserved to tell her side of the story.

"I received an interesting letter in the mail," he began.

Carla tipped back her coffee mug and set the empty glass on the porch railing. She leaned back in the swing and turned her attention his way.

"Do you know Lori Campbell?" he asked.

Her brows drew in and she shook her head. "Never heard of her," she replied.

"She passed away a month ago, but she left behind a letter." He kept his eyes on his mother. "For me." Sam didn't see any recognition in her eyes.

"Why are you telling me a dead woman left a letter for you?" she asked, then her eyes narrowed. "Did you get someone pregnant?"

"No, Mom. Lori was the mother of an associate of mine." *A brother.* "Her son is Nick Campbell. He's renovating the old building on Elkin Mountain and turning it into a resort in honor of his mother. She claims that Rusty Lockwood is my biological father."

The cigarette slipped from her hand, landing on

the concrete porch. His mother's eyes were wide, as was her mouth.

"Judging by your response, I'll take her letter to be accurate."

Pain sliced through him. She'd known this truth for over thirty years and chose to keep it from him. He'd never even been given the chance to decide what to do about his father, whether or not to seek out a relationship.

On one hand he understood her fear. His mother never would've been able to battle Rusty. But Sam could. He was.

"That man is a bastard," she ground out. "We were better off without him."

"We were, but there came a time when you could've told me the truth. I can handle it, mentally and financially," he added. "How much money did he give you to keep out of our lives?"

"Fifty thousand." She shifted in the swing and pushed her long black hair behind her ears. "I wasn't gambling so much back then and I was at least smart enough to invest half for your future. The other half I used to buy a reliable car and get a different apartment."

At least she'd thought to invest that money for him or who knows where he'd be. Sam was confident he'd still be a master distiller since that had been his goal, but would he have been able to put a down payment on the distillery he had now? Maybe not.

"I don't fault you for doing what you thought was best," he told her. "But there came a time when you needed to tell me the truth."

"And then what?" she demanded. "You would've gone to him and expected some grand reunion? You're in the industry. You know what an evil man he is."

Sam nodded. "I'm well aware."

Blowing out a sigh, Sam came to his feet and crossed to the railing. He curled his palms on the wood plank and stared out at the fog burning off the tips of the mountains.

"I don't know what the correct answer is," he finally stated. "But I know that I don't like finding out the truth and being blindsided by a stranger. And to find out he's my enemy. You know how much I hate that man."

The swing creaked and his mom's footsteps shifted across the porch as she came to stand beside him. She patted his hand and Sam knew this wasn't easy for her, either. Him coming here and confronting her was just as shocking as the truth was to him. She'd carried this secret for over thirty years.

"I worked for Rusty," she began. "I cleaned his house for about two months before our affair started. I was only eighteen and had no idea what I was going to do with my life, but then I fell for his charms and ended up pregnant."

Sam couldn't help but sympathize, knowing how

difficult that time must have been for her. A scared teen, legally an adult but with no direction—that had to have been terrifying.

"I was so naive," she mumbled. "I guess I thought he'd move me into that big mansion and we'd raise the baby together. I mean, to my knowledge he wasn't seeing anyone else. Of course I found out later he slept with everyone coming and going. The man had no scruples in business or in his personal life."

"So he offered you money and tossed you aside?" Sam guessed.

"Pretty much," she replied. "So I took that money and invested so you'd have enough to start a good life. Not like me. I wanted better for you."

Her voice broke on that last word and guilt had Sam turning and pulling her into his arms. She'd lost weight. His mother had always been a petite woman, but now she seemed almost frail. He'd have to keep a better eye on that because if she wasn't taking care of herself, then this addiction was even more out of control than he thought.

"I'm sorry I'm a disappointment," she murmured into his chest.

Sam eased back and wiped away her tears. "You've never been a disappointment. If I didn't love and care for you, I wouldn't be here. But you have to let me help you and you have to want help. It doesn't matter what I think of you. You have to love yourself enough."

She nodded and sniffed as she stared up at him with red-rimmed eyes. "I'm trying, Sam. I promise."

He knew this wasn't her life's goal; he knew she had aspirations. Nobody set out to become addicted to something. But he had to deal with the woman she was now. And he refused to let her continue down this rabbit hole of despair.

"I'm going to get your bills squared away and we're going to get you help," he told her.

"And Rusty? What are you going to do about him? He's such a powerful man."

Sam laughed. "He's an arrogant bastard who thinks he can bully his way around. I'm not worried about him and you shouldn't be, either."

She patted the side of his face, just like she'd done when he was young. "Be careful."

Be careful. Sure, no problem. Rusty was a nonissue. The man was on a downward spiral and wouldn't even be able to touch what Sam held dear.

Speaking of… Maty.

Being careful around Russ wasn't difficult, but watching his back where Maty was concerned was harder. Because they were far from over.

He'd barely gotten started with her.

Enemy or no, he'd gotten a sample of the woman she'd become and he wanted more.

Seven

After visiting his mother and putting in a full day of work, Sam was more than ready to unwind. Unfortunately, that was impossible with the thought of Maty on his mind.

The other night when she'd been in his home, her passion had been even more potent than he remembered. The way she didn't give a damn, the way she let him pleasure her...and the way she was more than ready to keep the intimacy going. Her raw honesty about what she wanted had humbled him and damn her, he hadn't been able to focus on much else since.

So here he was, heading toward the address he'd been surprised to find associated with her name...

an address he knew all too well. She hadn't said a word about her accommodations.

More secrets.

The area had once been thriving, but now this part of the valley had certainly seen better days. The apartment complex had gotten even more run-down than when he'd lived here as a teen.

Between his emotions from Maty's return and their very personal reunion, and this shocking revelation about where she was living, Sam had a sinking feeling that coming here was a mistake.

Wouldn't be the first one he'd made.

Sam turned into a parking lot with two sets of apartment complexes on each side. He glanced at each door for the familiar number and spotted Maty's car at the end, right in front of the place he'd called home for his entire childhood.

So she did live here. This wasn't just some error his assistant had made while digging around for the address.

Anger flooded through him. This had Rusty's slimy hands all over it and Maty was clearly the pawn. Sam had been furious with Rusty for hiring Maty, but now Sam was flat-out pissed. Whatever game Rusty was playing would be coming to an end because Sam would be putting a stop to it.

Taking advantage of his mother all those years ago and toying with Maty now was enough to make

Sam want to head straight to Lockwood Lightning and punch that man in the face.

He'd have to settle for getting even by keeping Rusty away from the distillery and everything else Sam held dear.

Sam parked next to Maty and stared at the door he'd walked through thousands of times as a child. He wasn't scarred by his childhood. His mother loved him unconditionally and poured herself into this tiny apartment. But that was a lifetime ago and being back seemed surreal.

He wondered how Maty felt when she came back to this town and lived in a run-down apartment building. What had happened to her job in Virginia? What had happened to her family's money?

Sam had no idea, but Rusty did and likely that's what he'd used as leverage to get her here. In order for Sam to properly help her, he needed the full story.

After Sam locked his truck, he made his way up the cracked sidewalk to the chipped black door. Nothing about this place was welcoming, but Maty had put a bright yellow wreath on the door to make her apartment stand out.

Sam tapped his knuckles on the frame and stepped back to wait. He heard muttering and bustling on the other side, and he kept his focus on talking to her and not exploding over why she let Rusty manipulate her into moving here…to this exact residence.

The chain rattled and a moment later the door

swung open. Maty's eyes widened. She held the phone to her ear and blinked away her shock before turning and walking back inside, leaving the door open for him. Sam took this as a silent invitation to enter.

"Just tell him I'll be there as soon as I can manage," she stated. "And make sure to tell him I love him."

Sam closed the door behind him as Maty disconnected her call. He examined the place, not knowing what to expect.

The old carpet had at least been replaced with some cheap vinyl faux wood flooring. There was one sofa, one chair, one lamp. No pictures on the wall, but there was a little throw pillow with flowers. A small glass jar sat on the two-person kitchen table. The jar held a bouquet of wildflowers that looked liked she'd plucked them from the side of the road.

The place was oddly familiar, yet different from the life he'd had here. A punch of nostalgia hit him, but he pushed it aside. Whatever mind game Rusty was playing, Sam wasn't going to get caught up in it.

"Why are you here?"

Sam turned his attention from his examination of the room to the woman who looked like she'd rather the grim reaper had shown up than Sam. Too bad. He wanted answers—he *deserved* answers.

"I thought I'd swing by on my way home and see if you wanted to get something to eat."

That lie rolled right off his tongue. He'd looked her up initially to see if they could pick up where they'd left off in his bedroom, but the moment he saw that address, he'd wanted answers.

She propped one hand on her hip and clutched her cell in the other. He also wanted to ask who she'd professed her love to, but that was none of his business.

Maty had clearly gotten home not long ago because she still wore one of those tight business dresses that reminded him of some naughty librarian fantasy with the way she had her hair pulled back.

But she'd kicked off her heels somewhere. Her bare feet shouldn't turn him on, but they did. Everything about her, from her appearance to her smart mouth to her vulnerability, seemed to be pulling him in…and that was before she'd come apart in his arms. Since then? Well, he was a mess of emotions he couldn't get a grasp on. He wanted her more now than ever.

"You stopped by unannounced to ask me to dinner?" She quirked a brow. "You're lying."

"Fine. I'm lying," he admitted. "I'm still hungry, so do you want to go get something?"

She quirked a brow. "You're not going to say anything about where I'm living?"

Sam ground his teeth and weighed his words. As much as he wanted to unleash his questions and anger, he also had to stop and think. Rusty was attempting to pull the strings and Sam was damn well going to be the one to cut them.

If Rusty had dug back into Sam's past to find this place, then likely Rusty knew Sam's mother's name, too. Did he remember her at all? Or was she just another woman in his past that he'd paid off and discarded?

"What do you want me to say?" Sam countered. He took a step toward her, noting her eyes as they raked over him. "All of this is part of Rusty's warped plan. He wants to get me thinking of our time together, remind me where I came from. Hell, I don't know what his angle is, but I know the end result he wants and he's clearly using you to get it. Do you want to tell me what he has over you?"

Her lips thinned. "I've already told you what I have going on with my client isn't something I can discuss."

"Considering I'm the common denominator, I'd think you could fill me in."

Maty blew out a sigh and reached up to her hair. She pulled out one pin, then another, until the mass of blond strands tumbled around her shoulders. She shook her hand through the waves and Sam's entire body tightened. He wanted to feel that silkiness over his body, through his fingers.

There was no doubt she just wanted to get more comfortable, but her actions seemed to border on seduction. The power she held over him now was different from that in their past. Sam was walking a fine line here, but he couldn't pull himself away from the little minx.

"Listen, I'm tired and cranky," she told him. "I just want to put on my leggings, take off my bra and do nothing."

Sam smiled. "Don't let me stop you from taking off your bra."

Maty rolled her eyes and turned toward the hallway leading to the bedroom. "That's such a man thing to say," she muttered as she disappeared.

Sam wanted nothing more than to follow her, but he didn't get the vibe she was in the mood for his shenanigans. He certainly could use something to take the edge off his mood. This bizarro world he'd found himself in with Maty and Rusty and his mother was taking its toll.

Keeping all the proverbial balls in the air was more of a full-time job than running a billion-dollar company.

When Maty came back moments later in black leggings and an off-the-shoulder tee, he gritted his teeth and clenched his fists at his sides. How could she look even sexier completely dressed down, with her face washed free of all makeup?

Because this was the Maty he remembered. Simply beautiful, casually elegant. She embodied everything he loved about women...curves and natural beauty.

"Are you going to just stand by the door or are you coming on in?" she asked.

"I haven't decided."

She crossed her arms over her chest, bringing attention to the fact she had indeed forgone the bra. Torturing him must be her hobby.

"Why did you decide to come see me to begin with?" she asked.

"I wanted to see you."

"You wanted to pick up from the other night," she corrected with a smile.

Sam shrugged. No need in denying the truth. He wasn't sorry he wanted her and he knew the feeling on her end was quite mutual.

"But now I want to know why you're here, in this apartment, and why you're letting Lockwood jerk you around."

She said nothing and Sam knew they would stand here and butt heads until one of them conceded…but neither was a quitter. She was just as strong willed as he was, which only added to the attraction that had nothing to do with their past and everything to do with the woman she was today.

He wanted to get to know that woman. He shouldn't, but he did. The last thing he had time for was getting tangled up in…hell, he didn't even know what to call all of this. There was no relationship—they hadn't even started a fling, though he didn't want to ignore that possibility.

After those sexy few minutes in his bedroom, he'd fantasized about her since. He'd bet his entire distillery on the fact that she'd been replaying those moments, too.

But it was that distillery that was at stake here.

At the end of the day, she still worked for his enemy, the one trying to take everything he'd dreamed of and worked for.

That didn't mean he couldn't enjoy her physically, though. It just meant he couldn't let anything develop beyond sex.

"Let me worry about my personal life," she told him.

Closing the distance between them, Sam reached up, sliding the pad of his thumb across the darkness beneath her eyes.

"You're exhausted and living in an environment that is much less than you deserve. Let me help you."

Her eyes never wavered. "Because you want in my bed."

"Wanting you in *my* bed has nothing to do with this," he countered, dropping his hand to her bare shoulder. "I don't like seeing you so worn down and being taken advantage of."

Before she could respond or argue, Sam took a step back. "Go get some shoes. I'm taking you to get something to eat."

She glanced down. "In case you missed it, I'm not dressed for going out."

Oh, he hadn't missed a thing about her...hence

the state of his constant arousal, and it wasn't taking her out in public that he wanted.

"Nobody will see you but me," he assured her.

Maty cocked her head. "Why does that sound dirty?"

He couldn't help but laugh. "If you're offering…"

She rolled her eyes and headed back toward her room. "Let me get my shoes."

A small victory, but he had a feeling the more time that passed without him knowing what was going on between Maty and Rusty, the deeper he'd be pulled into her world.

Was he playing right into Rusty's scheme? Was Maty in on this plan? He didn't think so, but at the same time, he hadn't seen her for sixteen years and here she was playing on his every emotion.

That was fine. There was no reason they couldn't pick up where they left off the other night. No reason they couldn't enter into a brief affair. They'd danced around this attraction for the past few days… the attraction that was only growing each time they were together.

Sam was taking back control of this entire ordeal and he would come out on top, unscathed and heart intact.

Maty shouldn't have been surprised when Sam turned into his driveway.

"Are you making dinner?" she snorted.

"Actually, my chef made up a variety of things earlier today, so you have your choice."

He pulled into his attached garage and the door closed behind them. Something about that closure had her pulling in a deep breath and wondering what would happen now. Sam was right that she was vulnerable and scared and being jerked around by Rusty, but telling Sam wouldn't fix the problem. If anything, it would only add to her issues because Sam would likely try to ride to her rescue.

She had to stand on her own, to find her footing in this new chapter of life. Falling back onto the man she'd once loved and left wouldn't be looking forward or helping her rebuild her life.

Maty would find a way to get all of this worked out so nobody got hurt. Well, she might get a few emotional scratches, but that was better than her brother not receiving the care he needed. She would do anything for him…he was the only family she had left.

Tears pricked her eyes. She hated being emotional, especially in front of Sam. Crying didn't solve anything and she didn't have time for the breakdown she desperately deserved.

Once upon a time, she'd had everything. Her family, a lucrative career, and she'd been only one rung away from making partner at the most prestigious firm in Arlington, Virginia.

All of that changed in the span of a year when her parents died, her brother was injured and Rusty blackmailed her.

Here she was at rock bottom, back in her hometown, and the one man she didn't want to see her at her absolute worst was now the one man she wanted to lean on the most.

When he stepped out of the truck, Maty patted her eyes and opened her door. Sam was already there, reaching for her hand.

"You want to talk about the tears?" he asked, his broad frame blocking her from exiting.

Nothing ever got past the man. He'd always been so in tune with her feelings and emotions when they'd been together before. Perhaps that was just a by-product of being raised by a single woman.

"Not particularly," she replied. "Do you want to talk about your bad day?"

Sam's lips twitched. "Let's go see what my chef prepared."

Clearly they were at a standstill. Fine by her. The less personal involvement they had, the better in the long run. Orgasms didn't count.

Maty followed him into the house. The kitchen had the largest concrete island she'd ever seen. She could appreciate this space more now than when she'd been here for the five-minute tour of the main floor and the hour up in the bedroom.

She took a seat at one of the sturdy wooden bar stools at the island and set her bag next to her. She watched as Sam bustled around in the fridge, pulling out various dishes.

"We're having a buffet," he told her as he continued searching. "Why don't you get into the wine fridge and grab something that interests you."

"You like wine?" she asked, going to the far wall that held an impressive-sized wine cooler.

He tossed a glance over his shoulder, his gaze raking over her. "I'm a connoisseur of all the fine things."

Yeah, they weren't just talking drinks anymore. As if she weren't on edge enough, adding in the impossible-to-ignore attraction certainly wasn't helping.

Maty chose a chilled Pinot and set it on the island. "Where's your opener?"

Sam grabbed some napkins and forks and nodded to the corner of the minibar. Maty spotted the electric opener and had the cork off in no time.

The view out the back patio doors was absolutely breathtaking. With the sun setting behind the mountains in the distance and the calm of the evening, Maty relaxed somewhat. Sam wasn't pushing for her to tell him things she couldn't and he wasn't trying to get her out of her clothes.

With her current state of anxiety, she wasn't sure

she could turn him down for either request too much longer. She desperately wanted someone to lean on, someone to offer her much needed advice. There was no one. Not anymore.

The people she spoke with the most were Carter's nurse and Rusty Lockwood. Neither of them were people she could confide in.

"If you keep looking like that, I'm going to think you hate my company."

Maty glanced over to Sam who stood with his hands resting on the edge of the island. She stared at the ridiculous display of food and couldn't stop the laugh.

"How hungry are you?" she asked.

"Starving—and you probably only had some gra-nola bar or microwave noodles for dinner."

Actually, she hadn't even made it to her microwave yet before he came, so he didn't know everything.

"Sit," he ordered, pulling out a leather chair that should have looked ridiculous at a dining table, but seemed masculine and fitting. "I'll make you a plate and pour you a glass of wine."

At this point she didn't care if he had ulterior mo-tives. The fact that someone was feeding her and supplying wine was all she needed to relax…even if just for a minute and even if she ended up in his bed.

Because she knew without a doubt that's where they were headed. Maybe not tonight, maybe not tomorrow. But Maty was certain that she wouldn't get out of Green Valley without landing in Sam Hawkins's bed again.

Eight

Sam had put away all of the leftovers, poured Maty another glass of wine and sent her into the library. She'd always been a bookish, artistic type. She'd been quite the artist when it came to pencil sketches and she'd always loved to read. His library had quite the variety of books and even an art desk in the corner. The room was tailor-made for her, though he'd never admit to any such thing if she asked him about it.

Right now, he wanted her to feel safe and calm. Something had bothered her today and he wanted her relaxed.

His own day had been a blow to the face, but at

least he knew the truth. Now he could move forward with the facts and use this knowledge as just another leg up over Rusty.

There was just so damn much to do. He needed to get his mother help, he needed to confront Rusty, and he needed to figure out how he and Nick were ultimately going to fight Rusty and win.

Then there was Maty.

Dealing with Maty sounded like a simple thing, when in reality she assaulted all of his emotions about every aspect of his life. She comprised a good piece of his past and was now settling all around his future. Having her back in Green Valley had thrown him off, but he couldn't say he was sorry.

And now she was back in his house because he couldn't just leave her be. Damn it, why did he have to care if Rusty was taking advantage of her?

He cared because he was nothing like his bastard father.

What would Maty say when she found out the truth?

Sam certainly admired her strong will, but at this point that hard head of hers was going to get her hurt and possibly damage her career. Rusty was still being investigated for illegal dealings and Sam didn't want Maty anywhere near that.

If the truth came out that Rusty was indeed stealing from the funds his employees set aside specifically for Milestones, a children's charity, Rusty

Lockwood would be finished…and so would anyone associated with him. Sam truly wanted Maty to have that career she'd left so long ago to achieve.

What happened to her family money? That question kept niggling at the back of his mind. Had she gotten involved in some scandal or made really poor financial choices? Something had happened to rip away the wealthy lifestyle Maty had grown up with.

Sam raked a hand over the back of his neck and headed from the kitchen toward the library. He stopped short at the open double doors. Maty had climbed up on the mobile ladder and was raking her fingertips along the spines of a series he'd never had a chance to read.

He couldn't help but admire her curves in those damn leggings and the way she reached had her T-shirt coming up and allowing him a nice glimpse of pale skin just above her waistband.

Gritting his teeth, Sam stepped in, making sure to slide his feet across the hardwoods to announce his presence and not frighten her.

"You've got quite a collection," she told him, still surveying her options. "I'm pretty sure I'd have to move my office to this room and never leave if I lived here."

If she lived here. That image hit him hard.

What seemed like a lifetime ago, they'd planned on living together. He'd had no money to offer, no home, but he would've done anything to give her whatever she wanted. He would've moved every obstacle, slain every demon to make her happy.

Yet she'd had other goals…goals that didn't include him.

Now, though, it seemed their roles had reversed.

Pulling a book from the slot, Maty glanced at the cover and carefully climbed back down. Sam crossed to see what she'd chosen.

"Historical," he muttered, looking at the title. "That always was your favorite subject."

She met his gaze. "History is so fascinating. That's how we got to where we are today. The culture, the laws."

Her intelligence had always impressed him, attracted him, and now was no different. There was so much similar about her, yet so many things had changed. How could he *not* want to get to know her more? To unveil each and every layer she'd added since leaving town?

"Do you always bring your ladies into your library?" she joked with a teasing smile. "Because I have to tell you, this room is a panty dropper."

Her face instantly shifted to a deep pink.

"Forget I said that," she quickly added. "I don't want to know what you do with women in here and I'm sure as hell not dropping my panties."

Sam tipped his head. "No? Well, that ruins all of my plans for the evening."

"You brought me here for sex? So predictable."

Sam shrugged. "I brought you here because I wanted some semblance of happy at the end of this terrible day. After I saw where you lived, I figured you'd want to explain how that happened. I'm trying to help you out of a situation I have no clue how you got into, and you're driving me out of my mind."

In so many ways. He wanted her physically, but he had to know what the hell she was hiding. Until he had all the ammunition on Rusty, moving forward was going to be the equivalent of walking through a minefield.

Maty let out a shaky sigh and turned. She crossed to the oversized desk beneath the long row of glass windows giving an impressive view of the mountains in the distance. She set her book down and shifted to lean against the edge of the desk.

Whatever war she was waging with herself, she clearly didn't want Sam as a witness. Too damn bad. He couldn't help her if he let her keep hiding…he'd been through that enough with his mother.

"Rusty offered me a job and a place to live if I came here," she told him as she crossed her arms over her chest. "I had no idea the place he had chosen was your old apartment until I arrived in town. I had nowhere else to go."

"Why didn't you just rent something else?" Sam asked. "I know a great Realtor who could hook you up with something in a better area, probably with some great views."

Her smile didn't quite reach her eyes. "Thanks, but I've got it covered."

Clearly she didn't have "it" covered or she wouldn't be in an apartment that was run-down and held memories for both of them. None of this made any sense.

Sam slid his hands into his pockets and kept his attention on her. The confidence and light he'd always associated with Maty didn't exist anymore. Even when she'd first called him, when he first saw her, she'd exuded that strength. But now…something, or someone, was pulling her down and he intended to find out what or who it was.

"What's Lockwood holding over you?" he asked.

She spun around to face him, that determined expression staring back at him, but there was still an underlying layer of fear. He could see it and he needed to penetrate that barrier she'd erected.

"Nothing I can't handle," she assured him with a smile that she clearly had to work for.

Sam took a step toward her. "You keep saying that, but you look exhausted."

"Well, if you'd sell your distillery to Rusty, then my stressful job would be over." She shrugged. "Do you want to discuss that?"

"Never."

"Then we're at a standstill."

Like hell they were. This interchange wasn't that simple or tidy. Frustration rolled through him and he knew there would be a good amount of time spent in his gym with the punching bag later.

"If you won't let me put you in touch with my Realtor to find you something you deserve, then get your things and move in here."

Maty stared at him, her eyes wide with shock. Hell, he'd surprised himself because the words had come out before he could fully think them through. But he wasn't sorry and had he given the idea more thought, he still would've said the same thing.

"I can't move in here, Sam. I work for Rusty and you and I are…we're…"

Sam slowly closed the distance between them, placing his hands on the desk on either side of her hips. "What are we, Maty?"

Her hands came up to his chest and she pressed against him. "Ease up there, pal. You're trying to make me say something that I'm not ready to admit."

Sam laughed and nipped at her lips. "Careful, babe. That lawyer side is starting to show."

"Because that's what I am before anything else," she replied. "My career is the one thing I have. It's my own and I have little else right now."

She'd lost so much, that was clear. But how?

Sam eased back, but not much. "So you've put your career before everything since you left? No relationships, no marriage?"

Her eyes darted away. "Nothing like that."

Interesting. That was a long time she'd been gone

and she'd never pursued a relationship? Not that he had gotten into anything serious, either.

"I mean, I dated," she amended. "I've had lovers."

He shouldn't be jealous, that was absurd. He hadn't been celibate for sixteen years so he knew she hadn't been, either.

And yet, he didn't want either of their past lovers to be dropped between them.

"Listen, don't make a decision right now," he told her…though he wanted her to say yes and just move in. "Think about it. You'll see staying here with me is for the best. You've seen how much room I have. You don't even have to see me if you don't want. If I'm the one helping you, then Rusty won't have a leg to stand on and can't hold anything over you."

And that was the gist of this entire situation. Sam wanted to be the one Maty needed.

A sad smile spread across her face. "You make it sound so easy, but that's not how reality works."

"Look—"

She held up a hand and eased away. "Why don't you tell me about how you came to be the youngest billionaire and master distiller in Tennessee."

She wanted a distraction from Rusty? Discussing Hawkins wasn't exactly the distraction he'd been thinking of, but it was his second favorite option.

"Fair enough," he agreed. "You know I always liked to experiment with beers when I was younger, but that wasn't where my passion was. I wanted more. When I was eighteen, my mother informed me that she'd invested a large sum of money when she found out she was pregnant with me."

Maty's eyes widened in surprise. "Wow. She did that? Um…sorry. I just never took her for someone to save."

Sam nodded. "No, it's okay. It's not like her gambling habit is a secret. She invested the money before her addiction really took hold."

"I didn't know you had that money when we were together," she told him. "Not that it matters."

"I didn't say anything because I didn't think of it as money I could use." Sam took a step and rested his hip on the back of a chair. "I'd been with her long enough to know one of us needed to be responsible and I didn't know when that money would be needed in an emergency."

Maty offered a smile as she tipped her head. "You always were mature for your age."

He had been, but he still hadn't been enough for Maty to stay. Now, though, he controlled his destiny, his relationships. Everything. He'd never let his defenses down again. Remaining in power over all aspects of his life was the only way to secure his heart.

"I tried bourbon at a tasting I went to and fell in love," he went on. "I knew that was what I wanted to do. Of course, there was much more that went into my start-up, but that's the dream I had and when I found out the old bourbon distillery in town was going to be sold, I knew that was my chance. The place hadn't been bringing in the profit it should've to keep running. I was literally in the right place at the right time to restart and all of the working equipment was there. I just had to use the funds that Mom invested. It was a risk because if I failed, we had nothing to fall back on. I poured my entire life into Hawkins from day one."

An idea sparked and he came to his feet and reached for her hand before he could talk himself out of this craziness. Why was he trying so hard for a woman who had shoved him aside years ago and wasn't letting him in now to help when she so desperately needed it?

"Do you trust me?" he asked.

Maty's brows rose as she laughed. "Should I not trust you? I'm the one keeping secrets."

"We all have secrets, Maty." And he wasn't ready to divulge his. He raked his thumb over the back of her knuckles. "Do you trust me?"

Her face instantly sobered and she nodded. "You keep asking me that. I trust you."

Those three simple words, said with such conviction, hit him hard. A sliver of hope speared him. Maybe, just maybe, he was getting through to her.

Here she was, stuck in the middle of a fight that had absolutely nothing to do with her. She deserved to know the truth, but at the same time, she wasn't exactly forthcoming with her own issues. So how the hell could he open up to her?

Sam squeezed her hand and smiled. "It's time for a field trip."

Maty had no clue what Sam had in mind when he'd mentioned a field trip, but sneaking in the back door of Hawkins Distillery certainly wasn't on the top of her list.

Well, she wasn't exactly sneaking since she was with the CEO, but it was dark and they hadn't used the main entrance.

"Isn't there a front door?" she asked as she stepped inside and Sam typed in a security code before flipping on the lights. "This feels very illegal."

Sam laughed. "I assure you, this is all very legal."

Maty glanced to the high ceilings, the large vats. Hoses seemed to run in all directions. The exposed brick walls added charm to the old building. All of the rustic areas mixed with modern day machinery seemed so Sam…a little rough around the edges, but polished.

"This building is amazing," she told him as she continued to survey the open space and the production area of the distillery.

"I figured you'd think so. It was built in the late 1800s." Sam moved around her and went to the far wall in the corner. "If you look here, they've marked when the flood came through in 1903."

Maty glanced up to where he pointed and noted the old plaque that had bronzed with age. She'd actually done a report in high school about that flood.

"This building was originally built as a hospital," she told him.

Sam nodded. "It was completely empty when William Wallace bought it to turn it into a distillery. When I purchased the place from him, we had to upgrade quite a bit for what I wanted, but the bones were here for me to work with."

Maty listened as he spoke with passion about not only his work, but also this building. He'd done so much, moving slowly to make sure he got things right before he opened the place up to the public for tours and tastings. He claimed he led several of the tours for years, without telling anyone he was the new owner. Maty loved that side of him, the side that was just an everyday guy who was doing what he loved.

Sam might be a billionaire, but he wasn't one who sat in an office all day. He truly loved every aspect of his work and it showed.

She followed him as he explained the process from the making of the mash to adding the yeast for fermentation. He explained how many hours or days everything had to wait between each step. The timing of a batch was crucial, even before it ever made it into a charred barrel.

"And you're about to unveil your first ten-year bourbon in a few months, right?" she asked.

Sam nodded. "That's one of the first things I did when I took over. I wanted to produce bourbon. That's been my ultimate goal. Our gin is the number-one seller in the country, third in the world. I'm hoping the bourbon takes off just the same."

Maty smiled. "I'm sure it will. You're Sam Hawkins. There's nothing you can't do."

His eyes ran over her. "There are some things that prove more difficult than others."

She held his gaze for a few silent, intense moments. Maty's attraction, and clearly Sam's, was only growing with each passing moment they spent together. Plus, seeing him here in his element, doing something he'd always wanted to do, really put things into perspective. He was even more attractive than she'd remembered. There was this new layer to him she hadn't fully gotten to know, but now that she saw yet another passionate side to him, she couldn't deny her growing feelings.

Sam had set out to do exactly what he wanted and he'd let nothing stand in his way.

Maty had always wanted to be an attorney, and she was. But now that Rusty Lockwood had entered the picture, he was stealing the joy from Maty's and Sam's dream careers.

How could the monster be stopped? Because Maty truly didn't see any way around him, and if she

confided in Sam, no doubt Sam would go straight to
Rusty and demand he release Maty from her con-
tract. Then where would her brother end up? Maty
sure as hell didn't have the funds to help him, not
anymore.

Her brother hadn't had insurance, so after the fu-
neral expenses were paid for, the remainder of their
inheritance had gone to medical bills. Maty had sold
the family home and used that money as well. Her
job had kept her going for only so long before more
medical bills started coming in.

Little by little, she'd lost her grip on the life she'd
built for herself. She'd sacrificed her relationship
with Sam to make her career dreams come true—
now look at her. She was on the brink of losing everything and that initial sacrifice had all been in
vain.

"Show me more," she stated after a while, wanting to focus on something positive and because she
was actually so proud of Sam. "Do you have the
bottles ready to go for the new bourbon?"

Sam's lips quirked. "We do, but those aren't being
unveiled yet."

"Not even to me?"

He crossed to her and slid his hand over the small
of her back, guiding her through the maze of equipment. "Especially not to you."

Because she worked for Rusty.

She had to understand where Sam was coming

from, but that didn't mean his words hurt any less. She'd told him she trusted him, but he still didn't trust her. As long as she worked for the enemy, Sam would always have his guard up.

Maybe he'd have his guard up even without Rusty. After all, she was the one who had walked out. But…he hadn't even fought for her.

She'd always wondered if she would've given up everything for him, if he'd asked. But he'd been supportive of her dream and encouraging. How could she hate him for letting her go?

Damn those passive-aggressive thoughts. Nothing could change the past and she had enough of a mess with her present and future. There was no need to be looking backward.

"I can show you the warehouse where everything is stored," he countered. "But no pictures."

"I didn't even bring my purse or phone in," she replied.

Did he really think she'd take photos of everything here and send them back to Rusty? She wasn't that dedicated to the mogul. Her only loyalty came from ensuring her brother's health care, nothing more.

With Sam's hand on the small of her back, Maty was having a difficult time remembering why intimacy with him was a bad idea. Her body still zinged from that orgasm he'd given her days ago. Now here they were, in the evening, with not a soul around and all she wanted to do was strip out of these clothes and tell him to do whatever he wanted so long as it ended in pleasure for the both of them.

As they crossed the stone path that led to another building, Maty wanted more than anything to reveal the entire truth. She hadn't lied when she said she trusted him. She just didn't want him to think he had to save her. That was definitely not the attention she wanted from Sam. She didn't want his pity or his white knight rescue.

There had to be a way to make Rusty happy, allow Sam to keep his company, and keep her brother in the right care.

"You ever have bourbon?" he asked as they reached the old stone building with a modern metal door.

"I tried brandy once." She turned to face him and smiled. "I honestly thought it tasted like lighter fluid."

Sam laughed. "I'll ignore the fact that you've never had lighter fluid and just say that not all bourbons are the same and they definitely are quite different from brandy."

"I promise to try Hawkins when it releases."

Sam's hands came up to rest on her shoulders. "Maybe we can work out a deal where you get your very own complimentary bottle."

Maty couldn't help herself. She was going to play along.

The shadows across Sam's face seemed to make him menacing, mysterious. But she knew him. Even after all this time, she knew him.

"What did you have in mind?" she asked, knowing she had ventured into the "playing with fire" category.

There was this pull to Sam, stronger than the pull when they'd been younger. She found him even more fascinating, more powerful, more everything than sixteen years ago. He'd set his sights on a goal and nothing had stood in his way—not even losing her.

Confidence and integrity were serious turn-ons for her and Sam had all the qualities she loved in a man. Too bad she couldn't have this man back in her life.

Maty was so damn proud of him, especially considering his background. While she'd had all the makings for a successful future, her world had still crumbled. The instant her parents and brother were in that accident, Maty had found herself spiraling down a black hole.

No matter what, she intended to claw her way out and land back on her feet again without begging anyone for help.

"I'm sure we can think of some way for you to get an exclusive bottle," he promised with a wink.

"Sexual?" she asked.

Sam shrugged. "If that's what you want."

"I'd rather buy a bottle than be gifted one after sex."

"Then why did you bring it up?"

Maty glanced away, afraid her emotions would show. "I assumed that's where you were headed with your thoughts."

He smoothed her hair back and framed her face, forcing her focus back to him. "I respect you a hell of a lot more than to exchange booze for sex, Maty. And any man who would treat you in such a demeaning manner should have his balls kicked up to his throat."

"Ouch," she cringed.

"I'm serious."

Those dark eyes held hers and she knew he took her welfare very seriously…that was part of the issue and the entire war she waged with herself. She'd love nothing more than to dump her problems on someone else and tell them to fix them. But that's not how she was raised and she was much stronger than that.

Sam leaned in and nipped the sensitive spot just below her ear, then stepped back, but he settled his hands on the dip in her waist. Shivers spread all through her as she stared back at him.

"What was that for?" she asked.

"Because I know you like that spot…or you always did, and I want you to know that I'm here. No matter what's going on with you and Rusty or whatever it is you're afraid to tell me, I'm here if you decide you need someone."

Maty's throat burned with emotion and she willed

herself not to cry at his genuine words. How easy would it be to fall back into that comfort zone with Sam? Even though they had changed over the years, he still understood her.

But there was still so much standing in the way of her and Sam. The possibility of a relationship was so far-fetched, it seemed virtually impossible. She'd walked out on him once and was now working for his enemy.

But, one thing stood out above all else. She wanted Sam with a fierceness she was done denying. There was no reason she couldn't push those conflicts aside just for one night.

Tonight, she was taking what she wanted.

Nine

Sam had no clue what had come over Maty.

She had wrapped herself around him, plastering her body against his, kissing him like she'd been waiting the entire sixteen years to do so.

Sam gripped her backside and pulled her pelvis against his as he returned the passionate kiss. They'd been working up to this since that first moment she'd strolled into his office. She was too damn smart, too damn sexy, too damn…emotionally out of his reach.

Except now. And wasn't that what he wanted? The physical?

Sam sure as hell didn't have time to nurture a relationship. Hell, he was taking care of his company, his mother, getting started with a new brother, and maybe another... Then there was Rusty.

Not someone Sam wanted to filter through his mind while he had a handful of Maty.

Sam released her mouth, but nothing else.

"Why now?" he asked, trying to catch his breath.

She licked her lips and Sam's entire body tightened in response. He started walking her backward while she spoke.

"Because I want this," she told him as she nipped his chin. "And because, for tonight, I want to forget all the secrets and all the fears and every outside source that's telling me this is a mistake."

Fears. He knew she had them and he wanted more than anything for her to lay them all on him so he could protect her. But once again she was putting her career ahead of him. He expected nothing less, but that didn't mean he had to like it.

Why wouldn't she let him help? Yet another topic he didn't want to settle between them...

He wanted nothing more than to erase everything and everyone except this moment right here.

As he urged her into the warehouse, he quickly glanced away from her and punched the code before turning on a minimal amount of lighting and locking the door behind them. The hour grew later, they were alone, but he wasn't taking any chances.

Sam lifted her until her legs locked around his

waist. He carried her to the side where an old bench sat next to the door.

"Is this part of the tour?" she asked with a smile.

"You're getting the exclusive VIP."

He sat her down and before he could reach for her clothes, she had her hands on his jeans. He wasn't about to stop a woman who clearly knew what she wanted. To know she was still so passionate, so ready for this, only turned him on even more.

The moment she jerked his pants and boxer briefs down, Sam reached behind his neck and grabbed a fistful of T-shirt and yanked it over his head.

Sam turned them and sat on the bench. Then he looked up and his eyes locked with hers. He'd never seen a more beautiful sight. Her lids were heavy with desire, her lips swollen from his. There was no hesitation, nothing that made him think she'd have regrets later. She had the slightest smile, a strand of hair had fallen over her forehead and down onto her cheek. She kept her attention on him as she peeled out of her clothes. One garment at a time, she performed the simplest, sexiest striptease until she stood before him completely bare.

"Get my wallet, back of my pants, and get out protection," he demanded.

When she bent over to retrieve the condom, Sam took every single second to admire her curves, her creamy skin. When she stood back up and shook her hair away from her face, Sam couldn't stop himself from reaching for her.

He gripped her hips and tugged her forward. "Put it on me," he growled, anticipation consuming him.

Maty tore open the package and rolled the protection into place. Sam gritted his teeth at her intimate touch. He'd never thought he'd be with her again. The possibility had never entered his mind. But now that she was here, he was going to take in every single moment...because this time might be the last.

They were using each other tonight. He wasn't naive anymore. She didn't want to be with him beyond sex, and he couldn't be with her after this, either. There was no happily-ever-after for them, like he'd assumed their first time around.

But he sure as hell wasn't going to turn away this sultry vixen as she started to straddle his lap. Maty's fingers curled around his shoulders as she stared down at him. He always liked to think he was in control, but at this moment, he was utterly powerless. Maty could do whatever she wanted and he would be more than willing to sacrifice his body to be her playground.

"Touch me," she demanded.

Sam filled his hands with her breasts—he replaced one hand with his mouth. The moment he covered her, she sank down and joined their bodies. Maty cried out and jerked her hips, urging Sam on even more. He was so consumed by this woman, watching her come undone all around him had to be the most erotic moment of his life.

True, they'd been together before, but nothing had prepared him for this very captivating version of his Maty.

Before those last two words could freak him out or cause him to worry, Sam curled his fingers around her hips and let himself go. She smoothed his hair back, rested her forehead against his, and pumped her hips in a way that made him go out of his ever-loving mind. She murmured something he couldn't quite make out, but he wasn't trying, either.

His body trembled for quite some time, and he was in no hurry to come out of this euphoric state. Having Maty enveloping him, having his every sexual fantasy come to life right here in his warehouse…this was much more than he'd ever expected.

"Is the tour over?" she finally asked.

Sam wasn't near ready to take her back. He palmed her backside and gave an arousing squeeze.

"We're just getting started," he promised.

Sam shoved his hands in his pockets and walked through the alley to meet Nick at the back door to the bar where Rusty and his cronies were inside for their weekly card game.

The sun hadn't quite set, but the taller building

cast a shadow onto the narrow space. Nick waited outside the door and nodded as Sam approached.

"Does this all seem different now?" Sam gestured between them. "This truth is still processing."

Nick shrugged. "We're still the same people and thankfully neither of us are like that asshole in there."

Sam laughed. "True."

"Nothing is stopping me from bringing him down," Nick stated. "Knowing that you're my brother and in my corner only makes me more determined. You can get moonshine anywhere around here, but I want gin, bourbon, scotch… I want it all. My patrons deserve options and not to be limited… Never mind. I know you understand, I just get so pissed going around and around with this damn game Rusty is playing."

Sam listened and completely got where Nick was coming from. Rusty was the epitome of a bully and the man didn't give a damn who he hurt or stepped on, so long as at the end of the day, he continued to rake in the millions he believed he deserved.

"Listen, now that we both have more ammunition on him, we can really put the screws to Rusty," Sam stated. "You know his time is limited and he's not going to be able to keep up his monopoly on this area. Younger, smarter, much more powerful people are coming up and not backing down at his demands. He doesn't know how to handle that."

Nick nodded. "No, he doesn't. He called me the other day and asked me to reconsider exclusively serving his moonshine at the resort. He said he'd even work on a special batch just for my place."

Sam grunted. "I'm sure he would offer anything to a new resort that has so much buzz around it."

Which was why Rusty wanted his hand in all the distilleries, namely Hawkins—because of all the buzz.

"Well," Nick stated. "My assistant sent some informative stats to the city council members regarding the amount of revenue that would come into each restaurant and hotel should the liquor licenses open up."

Sam crossed his arms and rocked back on his heels. "Smart. Lockwood can't hold on to this stranglehold forever. His time is limited."

"I agree and we're just pushing this right along," Nick added with a smirk.

"I'm about finished with being subtle and nice," Sam stated as he nodded toward the closed door. "Let's go play some poker."

Before Sam could take a step, Nick held up his hand. "Everything okay?" he asked.

Sam sighed and wondered how Nick knew something else was on his mind. He'd taken Maty back to her place last night after she'd completely blown his mind in the warehouse. He hadn't mentioned her moving in with him again, but he hoped the seed had been planted and she'd seriously consider it.

What irked him now was that the idea had taken root in his own mind. He actually wanted her in his house.

In the beginning, he'd wanted her there to take the control away from Rusty, because if Maty was under Sam's roof, then he had more leverage to help her and find out what the hell she was hiding.

But now...

Damn it, now he wanted her there for all those reasons and so much more. He wanted to protect her, he wanted her to feel safe and to stop this battle she would never win, and he wanted her in his bed.

"Woman troubles?"

"I don't have a woman, but I have problems," Sam stated honestly. "Let's deal with this problem first. Rusty has been a pain in my ass for years."

"Then let's see if we can't push this along," Nick said as he reached for the door handle. "When all this is wrapped up, maybe you'll want to let me in on the woman you claim you don't have."

Maybe he would. Maybe having a brother would reveal a whole new set of emotional doors, ones that would open up opportunities for Sam to move forward and trust others again.

All of that, including Maty, would have to be dealt with later. Right now, he had a poker game to attend.

Ten

"But that's not possible," Maty cried into her phone as she slammed her car door. "Carter's care is paid up for another month."

"I'm showing an email that states his stay and medical assistance will be terminated at the end of next week, but I wasn't given any indication on where he will be moved," the director of the facility stated. "I'm sorry to call so late, but I was working on some reports and was surprised to see this change since Carter has only been here a short time. I was hoping you could let me know where he's headed so we can contact the new facility and get the paperwork started."

Maty gripped her phone in one hand and fished her keys from her bag with the other. She had no idea what was going on, but she knew exactly who was holding the purse strings.

"Can I call you back?" Maty asked as she shoved open her door...or tried to because the damn thing kept getting stuck. "There's just been a misunderstanding and I'll get this squared away."

"Yes, of course. Thank you."

Maty disconnected the call and shoved her shoulder against the door to get the damn thing to open. Once she was in, her mind was racing. She didn't give a damn that it was late on a Friday night, she wanted some answers.

She dropped her purse on the table inside the door and immediately dialed Rusty. Of course the call went to voice mail. He could never be bothered to answer his cell, not even for her. He always called her back after he'd seen the missed call.

Maty shot off a text that she needed to speak with him and it was an emergency. Why in the hell had he messed with the payments? Why had he informed them that Carter wouldn't need a room after next week? There was nowhere else for her brother to go and without insurance or money up front, nobody would take him.

Part of her wanted to cry for being put in this position, but the practical side of her knew that nothing would be solved if she cried. Time was not on her side and she had to find some answers, then she had to find a solution.

She stared at her phone, willing it to ring. Frustrated, infuriated and beyond exhausted, Maty grabbed her bag and headed back out the door. She didn't even think about her next move, she simply got in her car and drove to Sam's house.

She hadn't seen him since he'd dropped her off at her apartment last night after her VIP tour of the distillery.

At this point, she wasn't sure what to say to him, at least not about their intimacy. What could be said? They clearly didn't have an issue with sex—granted that had never been a problem, but they weren't young and in love anymore. She had a serious problem and there was no way to get help unless she laid out her cards.

Which was how she found herself pulling into Sam's drive a few minutes later. These rash decisions weren't typical for her, but desperate times and all that.

Tears pricked her eyes, and she blinked them away as she pulled up to the steps of Sam's home. The moment she put the car in Park, the skies opened up and rain poured down. Groaning, Maty reached into her door pocket for her mini umbrella. She shoved open her door and attempted to gather her purse while opening the umbrella.

The damn thing wouldn't budge. She jerked at it

one more time, but her hip bumped the side of the car and she closed the door on her purse.

Rain pelted against her as she jerked open the door and tugged her purse free to bang against her side. Once the door was closed, she finally got the umbrella up as she started toward the stone steps leading to the porch. A gust of wind caught her off balance and the umbrella jerked inside out.

Cursing, she tossed the damn thing into the landscaping and raced up the steps. Sam was probably inside laughing at her this entire time, nursing some tumbler of bourbon, while she stood out here soaking wet and shaking off the excess moisture like a dog.

It was then she realized the dampness on her face was rain mixed with tears. Angry tears, fearful tears, worried tears—she had them all and they weren't stopping anytime soon. There was only so long she could hold it together and she'd reached her breaking point.

She pressed the doorbell and waited, swiping the moisture from her face. After a moment, she used the door knocker and waited. And waited.

Damn it. She should've called or texted instead of assuming he was home. Where was he? Not like he had to check in with her or anything, but she needed him to be here. She needed to get this process moving. After the phone call she'd just had, there was no time to waste.

Furious, Maty pulled out her cell from her purse and dialed Rusty again. She left yet another message and then tossed the phone back into her bag and glanced around the porch. Rain continued to beat down and she eyed the broken umbrella in the landscaping. She was positive there was some resemblance between that damn thing and the shambles her life had become.

No matter, her first priority was to make sure her brother's care continued and he remained exactly where he was.

A rumble of thunder rolled through and Maty crossed to the porch swing. She wasn't going anywhere until she talked to Sam. A call from Rusty would be better, but she had to be more proactive than ever before.

Maty pointed her toe onto the porch floor and pushed off to send the swing swaying. Her mind traveled back to when she and Sam would lie in the back of his truck bed on a sleeping bag and stare up at the stars. They'd discuss the future, one they'd assumed they'd spend together. He'd always said he'd have a porch swing. He'd always told her he'd make a name for himself, to be someone she'd be proud to call hers.

But her goals had ultimately pulled her away from him and no matter how much she'd tried to make everything work, having a long-distance boyfriend while attending law school hadn't been ideal.

She couldn't give up her life's goal to study law for young love any more than Sam could give up his goals to follow her to law school. If she'd stayed and ignored what she'd truly wanted, she would've ultimately resented Sam. Maybe she should've tried to find her way back, but she'd been away so long fulfilling her obligations that she hadn't been sure how to try again.

She'd never wanted to hurt him and yet here she was, ready to hurt him all over again, but this time she had no choice.

Rusty wasn't backing down and he was forcing her hand by stopping the funding for Carter's care.

No matter what her feelings were for Sam, in the past or now, she had to promise him anything to get him to sell Hawkins. Her brother's well-being depended on it and her heart would just have to break again.

The poker game could've been worse. Sam was out only a few hundred bucks, but Rusty hadn't been in attendance. Perhaps he had something else to do, but Sam figured the old bastard was just avoiding him.

Even with Rusty's absence, Sam and Nick came away with a victory. A little chatter amongst the city council about the new resort and the new bourbon launch this fall was more than enough to pique their interest in revisiting how they approached liquor licenses.

Sam adjusted his wipers to a faster speed as he pulled into his drive. The lights slashed across the concrete and the trees flanking either side of the drive. His mind rolled from one thought to another, from one issue to the next.

Maybe he could have everything he wanted. The licensing opened up to where he could supply his own hometown with his own creations, ruining Rusty Lockwood...*and* he could have Maty.

He hadn't spoken to Maty yet today and he knew she had to be thinking of last night just the same as he was. Every touch, every kiss. Each moment kept playing through his mind. He wanted her to move in with him now more than ever.

As he approached his house, he spotted her red car in front of his porch. Sam pulled into his garage and, instead of going into the house and out the front door, ran up the stony path through the rain toward the porch. He did a quick glance toward her car to see if she was sitting inside, but he didn't see her. He did, however, spot a broken umbrella lying in the middle of his buttonbush.

The second he raced up the steps, he spotted her...asleep on his porch swing. The rain continued coming down in sheets and thunder rolled in the distance.

Sam swiped the rain from his eyes and raked

a hand over his hair to get rid of the moisture. He didn't dare move closer. She looked so damn peaceful, even with those dark circles beneath her eyes. He wanted to erase any sign of stress or fear from her life. He wanted to give her everything she'd been robbed of…for reasons he still didn't understand.

Strands of honey hair had fallen over her shoulder and rested against her cheek. She still had on her shoes, her cell was clutched in one hand, but her purse was on the porch floor.

Had she been waiting on a call?

Sam pulled his cell from his pants and glanced to the screen. She hadn't called or texted him.

Did this mean she wanted to discuss moving in or had she just shown up for a repeat of last night?

He wouldn't mind both, actually.

Sam went to the front door, typed in the code to unlock it and reached inside to disarm the security system before turning his focus back to Maty. He took her purse and set it inside the entryway on the table, then he came back out. There was no way to avoid disturbing her sleep, but maybe he could make this as easy as possible for her.

He slid one arm around her shoulders and the other beneath her knees and scooped her up against his chest. Her phone fumbled a little in her hand, but ultimately landed where their bodies joined. Maty stirred, but her eyes remained closed as her head lolled toward him.

She was dead tired and working herself like a damn racehorse for a jackass who was using her. Sam still wasn't sure what was going on, but he knew Maty would literally break before admitting weakness.

As he carried her into the house, he knew full well that she wasn't weak. She never had been. This woman was one of the strongest he'd ever known and her coming back here, attempting to take on Sam as an opponent, just proved how strong willed she was. When faced with a losing battle, she still pressed on, determined to win.

How could he not admire her? How could he not find her strength so damn sexy?

The cell buzzed between them and Sam stopped before he could mount the steps. Maty's eyes flew open and she started moving to the point where he was afraid he'd drop her.

Carefully, he set her down and held her phone out to her, but not before he saw Lockwood's name on the screen.

Son of a bitch. The man had the absolute worst timing—not that there was ever a good time for Rusty to cause an interruption, but it was like he knew when to be the biggest pain and he reveled in the moment.

Maty grabbed the cell and swiped her hair from her face. She glanced around like she wasn't sure how she'd gotten into his house, but then she answered the call and turned her back to Sam.

Considering this was his house, he wasn't going anywhere and he'd be damned if he'd give her privacy right now. He reset the alarm and waited, knowing this call could be key in helping him figure out what was going on.

"What the hell are you doing to me?"

Sam was shocked at the way she answered the phone, but those words only confirmed exactly what he'd thought, what he'd been afraid of. That gut feeling grew deeper, the ache of realizing whatever Rusty held over her must be pretty bad for her to have such a reaction.

"You're playing a game with his life," she cried as she started for the steps.

Sam thought she was going to go up, but she reached up with a shaky hand and held on to the banister. Slowly, she turned to sit on the second stair. Her fingers curled around the wrought iron and she rested her head against her hand. Weariness and frustration radiated from her and Sam wanted to slay every damn dragon she faced—especially if they shared the same dragon.

But at this point he still didn't know what exactly he was up against.

"You ask the impossible," she murmured.

When her voice cracked on that final word, Sam

had heard enough. He crossed to her, grabbed the phone from her hand and disconnected the call.

"Sam," Maty cried as she sprang to her feet. "You can't do that."

"I just did," he countered. "I'm not going to let that bastard continue to beat you down. What the hell is going on?"

Of all the reactions he expected, tears welling up in her eyes was not one of them. Her face crumbled as she turned away on an audible sob. He honestly expected her to fight him, to argue or grab her cell and call Rusty right back. He expected her to ignore his demand, but he'd not expected her to emotionally break down.

All the more reason to end this cycle of fighting and get her to talk to him. Everyone had a breaking point and Maty had obviously just reached hers.

Sam shoved her cell into his pocket and closed the narrow distance between them. Gripping her shoulders, he pulled her back against his chest and waited for her to say something. As much as he wanted answers, he didn't want to see her hurting. Nothing was worth her pain, not even him gaining more leverage over Rusty.

Maty's body shook and the racking sobs absolutely broke him.

Turning her, Sam lifted her in his arms once again and carried her up the stairs.

"I'm not staying," she sniffed. "Sex isn't why I came."

He said nothing as he continued up to his master suite. He'd have to be a completely heartless jerk to assume she was ready for anything other than shelter. That's all she needed at this point. Shelter from Rusty, from herself, even from Sam. She needed to feel safe and damn it if he wasn't going to be the one to give her the haven she needed.

"I can't stay here," she muttered, the fight literally draining from her voice. "I have to fix this. You have to... I'm sorry. You have to sell the distillery. I know how hard you've worked and it's your passion. But please."

Like hell. He wasn't selling. He wasn't letting Rusty trample all over her, and he sure as hell wasn't letting any of this continue another day.

Sam stepped into his room just as a flash of lightning lit up the glass of the balcony doors. He laid her on his bed and smoothed her hair from her face. Reaching over, he clicked on the small accent lamp on the nightstand and sank down on the edge beside her hip.

Her watery eyes stared up at him. "I don't have time for this," she told him. "I have to make sure Carter stays where he is."

Carter? What did her brother have to do with this entire ordeal?

"You're not making sense, sweetheart."

She closed her eyes and pressed her fingertips to her forehead. "My brother needs medical care. I can't afford it anymore."

"Medical care for what?" Sam asked, leaning down closer to hear her mumbles.

"The wreck that claimed my parents." She opened her eyes and focused on him once again. "That wreck left my brother paralyzed, and he needs twenty-four-hour care. Governmental aid isn't enough to cover the high-quality care he needs. He's at River Bend in Arlington right now."

Paralyzed. Damn. Why hadn't she told him that before? Why hadn't he searched deeper into her past to figure out what was going on? He knew she'd battled something, but he'd been too consumed with his own issues, too distracted by his reaction to having her back in his life that he hadn't gone that extra step.

Because he'd been consumed with seeing her again and he'd been rendered useless by his hormones.

Now here she was, clearly being manipulated by Rusty in a way Sam had never imagined and in a more infuriating way than he'd expected.

"Rest," he told her, hoping he could make her realize he wasn't the enemy. "I'll take care of it."

Her eyes widened with fear. "No. You can't."

"I will," he assured. "You said the other night that you trusted me. Now is the time to put that trust to the test."

She started to sit up, but Sam placed his hands on her shoulders and eased her back down. She wasn't going anywhere tonight…or for a long time if he had his way about it. She needed to find a place where she could rest and recover. Self-care was something he insisted his employees take time for and Maty was a hell of a lot more important in his life than they were…more important than he wanted to admit even to himself.

"Trust me," he murmured, staring straight into her worried eyes.

"Don't take on Rusty," she pleaded. "He's awful, Sam. You can't get mixed up with him."

Too late.

"I'm taking over," he told her, placing a kiss on her forehead. "Don't worry about your brother, Lockwood or even yourself. It's all on me now and I swear to you, this will all be taken care of."

Every single bit. He hadn't been able to fix their relationship in the past, but he sure as hell could fix her situation now. There was no money, no powerful man, absolutely nothing that would prevent him from making all of this right for her.

He would take on Rusty and it would be a damn pleasure to ruin the bastard. Father or not, Rusty Lockwood's reign of bullying and controlling was officially over.

Eleven

Hands roamed over her hip and down to the dip in her waist. Maty arched, relishing in the promising, arousing touch.

That talented hand moved around to the front, teasing the edge of her panties at that most sensitive spot high on her inner thigh. Her hips jerked just as the fresh aroma of coffee overcame her.

Coffee? Who the hell was making coffee at a time like this?

Maty blinked, focusing on the foreign room.

Oh, no. No, no, no.

She was in Sam's bedroom and Sam's hand wasn't on her at all.

"Don't let me stop you."

Her own hand had been teasing the edge of her lacy panties, but she'd clearly been dreaming that touch belonged to Sam…and she'd been caught.

Maty jerked around to see him standing at the end of the bed, mug in hand, naughty grin on his face.

Why did she have to be dreaming about the man while in his bed without him? Couldn't she just have a fantasy in private?

Maty grabbed the sheet and yanked it up over her waist.

"Where are my clothes?" she asked.

He moved around to her side of the bed and extended the mug. "I removed your shoes and pants after you fell asleep. I figured you should be comfortable. I assure you, you're the only one who did any touching of that body."

Maty rolled her eyes and sipped the coffee.

"I assume you still take vanilla creamer and sugar."

She eyed him over the rim. "You keep vanilla creamer?"

Sam shrugged. "I bought it yesterday since I asked you to move in the night before."

"Should I be impressed that you remembered my coffee order?" she asked, ignoring the topic of her moving in.

"I impressed myself," he told her with a wide grin. "You hungry?"

Damn it. He was being all cute when she just wanted to be angry. But she wasn't angry with him. She was angry at herself for being caught in this trap to begin with and for showing so much vulnerability by coming here in the first place.

"Do you want to get down to business or do you want to get breakfast first?" he asked.

She clutched the sheet and narrowed her eyes.

"I appreciate the invitation, sweetheart, but by business I meant discussing your brother and Rusty."

That got Maty's attention. She glanced around for her phone.

"I need to—"

"You need to do nothing," he told her. "Your brother's care is paid for through the next five years."

Maty gasped as she stared back at Sam. "What?"

"I called first thing this morning and spoke to a wonderful lady named Pearl and she was all too helpful and delighted that Carter would continue his care at River Bend." Sam sat down next to her, took the mug from her hands and placed it on the nightstand. "So, that's taken care of for a while. Is that all that Lockwood held over you? I'm assuming you had to get me to sell or he was cutting off funds for your brother? I am still trying to figure out what happened to your money, though I'm assuming funerals and medical bills wiped you out."

Maty couldn't believe what she was hearing. The cost of Carter's care for one year alone was staggering and he'd paid for *five* all before she'd even had her first cup of coffee.

He'd also figured out each and every one of her puzzle pieces and put them together like an expert. He wouldn't have gone to all that trouble if he didn't care…would he?

Still, as grateful as she was, she was also embarrassed that she couldn't take care of her own family… her *only* family.

"I—I don't know when I can repay you," she admitted, humiliated that she couldn't even stand on her own two feet right now.

"You're not repaying me anything, ever." Sam laid his hand over hers. "Now would be a good time to say thank you and then tell me you're moving in so Rusty doesn't hold anything else over your head."

"What?"

He shook his head. "That came out wrong. I didn't help your brother as leverage to get you to live here. I helped because he needs the best care and I don't want Rusty to have any more power over you. He might be an asshole but the facility he paid for is one of the best, which I'm assuming is how he kept blackmailing you."

"How do you know it's so good?" she asked.

He leveled his gaze on her and Maty knew he'd obviously done some research while she'd been sleeping.

She didn't say a word. Sam was right and now

that he knew the truth, there was really no need for her to stay here. Maybe she should go back to Virginia to be with her brother, try to rebuild her life. She needed to find a job before Rusty made good on his promise and ruined her completely. At this stage in the game, she didn't have the means or the energy to fight him.

Maty pushed away from Sam and sat up. "I have to go," she told him, but he didn't budge. "Move, please."

"You don't have to go anywhere."

"I do. I can't—"

"Stay," he commanded. "Move your stuff in here and we can work this out."

Confused, Maty jerked. "Work what out?"

"You want to get back at Rusty for using you? Stay and help me take him down."

Maty studied his face. He was serious. Sam's jaw clenched as his stare held hers. She had never seen him this determined, this…almost angry.

"All because he wants to buy your distillery?" she asked. "That's what has you so upset?"

"My issues with Rusty go well beyond that," he replied. "I intend to see him pay no matter if you stay or not, but…stay, Maty. Just stay."

She'd never heard him sound so sincere. No, that wasn't right. He'd been extremely sincere when he'd asked her to stay the first time, when they'd been young. She hadn't been able to let herself even think about the possibility of staying the first time, but now…

Could she stay?

Could all of this be that simple? Or would Sam try to take over everything the way he'd handled these issues with Rusty? She'd prided herself on being independent for so long, but maybe it was time to admit she needed help. There was nothing shameful about being human and needing a hand.

And she couldn't deny Sam, not when her needs were too great, her heart becoming too involved.

Wanting a physical relationship with him was so naive, so not the place she was in her life right now, but here she was.

"Quit analyzing everything and just go with your gut," he told her. "When I asked you to stay, what was your first reaction?"

"Yes." She gripped the sheet in her hands. "My first thought was to ignore everything and say yes."

"Then say it now," he implored.

Maty closed her eyes and pulled in a deep breath. Why couldn't she? If her brother was safe, for a good amount of time now thanks to Sam, then Rusty had no hold over her. Sam would help her make sure Rusty didn't ruin her reputation to the point she couldn't get another job. She was free to do what she wanted…with whomever she wanted.

She'd meant it when she'd told Sam she trusted him. But did that trust extend to her heart?

Focusing on Sam's intense gaze once again, Maty swallowed. "And if I stay, then what?"

"We work to show Rusty that he can't manipulate people to get what he wants whenever he wants."

Sam seemed so intent on this plan…which made her realize that he held some animosity toward Rusty that had nothing to do with her. Whether she stayed or not, she had a feeling Sam would seek revenge and succeed in achieving it.

For messing with her life and her brother's, Maty was on board. Plus, how could she deny herself the one man she'd always wanted? Maybe she was a fool, but at this point, she really had nothing to lose. She had to make a fresh start sometime. Maybe it wouldn't work here, maybe it would. She'd never know if she didn't try.

"I'll stay," she told him. "For now."

The smile that spread across his face curled her toes and left nerves dancing in her belly.

What had she just agreed to?

A wave of relief washed over Sam. She was his… for now anyway. He hadn't thought much beyond getting her to agree, but he wasn't going to question anything.

Did he want her in his bed? Hell, yes. Did he want her to be where he could be reassured she was safe? No doubt.

Did he want something beyond all of that? Honestly, he was afraid to even let his mind travel down that path.

Right now, he had more on his plate than at any other time in his life. Moving his mother into a treatment program for her gambling addiction, playing games with Rusty, having a half brother, reuniting with the woman he'd fallen in and out of love with...

Just going down the list boggled his mind. Because on top of all of that, he had a distillery to run and a milestone bourbon launch to prepare for.

Which reminded him...

"Are you free next Friday?"

Maty blinked and leaned back against the pillows. "Friday? I don't think I'm busy. I mean, I need to figure out employment before Rusty has a chance to tarnish my name. He's too sneaky, so nailing him for slander might prove to be difficult and—"

"Rusty won't touch your reputation. Trust me." Sam would make damn sure of that. "So you're free Friday?"

She reached for her coffee and curled her fingers around the mug. If she had half the amount of confidence as she used to, she'd soon feel better about taking these next unknown steps.

"I'm visiting my brother sometime, but that's flexible. I can be free on Friday," she told him. "What's going on?"

"There's a private showing at Hawkins. Strictly for my high-end buyers and a few others I've invited to sample the bourbon that we will roll out in a couple months. It will be the first time anyone outside my elite group of employees has seen or tasted any of the ten-year bourbon."

He was both nervous and excited. He'd waited a decade for this moment…longer if he added in all the years he'd dreamed of becoming a master distiller.

"I want you there with me," he added, sliding a hand over her thigh.

She sipped her coffee and set it back down and stared at him a moment before letting out a snort of laughter.

"You want me to attend some open house, gala, VIP event when I was the one hell-bent on getting you to sell the entire company?"

He squeezed her leg through the sheet. "You were acting out of desperation because a man was blackmailing you."

"What do you think he's going to do when he finds out what all you've done?" she asked. "When he knows there's no more leverage over me and he's not going to get what he wants?"

"I can't wait until he finds out," Sam replied honestly. "I want him to realize he can't manipulate people, and he sure as hell can't have my distillery. He can make all the moonshine he wants, but I have a feeling his empire may be collapsing soon."

Lockwood Lightning had been under investigation for a month now regarding some embezzling when it came to the charity Rusty claimed to support financially. That was just another reason Sam wanted Maty away from that toxic man.

"I had nothing to do with his dealings with the charity," Maty told him. "When Rusty brought me on, he made sure to keep all other legal aspects private. My only job was to reconnect with you and find a way to get you to sell. He was willing to volley back and forth if you didn't agree to the amount he originally set."

"That's what someone like Rusty will never understand," Sam replied. "I'm not in this for the money, so no offer would've made me give up what I love."

Maty smoothed her hair back and pulled it over one shoulder. "I hate being used as a pawn," she complained. "I want to help you take him down for what he did to my brother and to me."

A plan formed faster than Sam could comprehend, but once the idea took root, he knew it was damn brilliant.

"Keep working for Lockwood," Sam suggested.

Maty nearly jumped. "What?"

"Let him think you have me considering an offer. I don't even care if you tell him you're staying here. Do what you think is best, but just make him believe things are going his way."

Maty's brows drew in as she tipped her head to the side. "Are you using me?"

Sam shifted on the bed until he had both hands resting on either side of her head and he was within a breath of her face.

"Never," he promised. "If you don't want to be part of this or if you want no more dealings with him, I'll make sure you never have to worry about him again. Just say the word."

Her wide eyes studied him. "No. I'm all in with you."

And because he was this close and she looked too damn sexy rumpled in his bed, he slid his lips over hers for the briefest of moments.

"I'll never use you, Maty, and I won't let anyone else use you, either."

He kissed her again, this time coaxing her lips apart because he wanted more…he needed more.

Her fingertips feathered over his arms and onto his shoulders as she pulled him in deeper. Sam eased up further onto the bed until he lay mostly on top of her. He was careful to keep his weight shifted so he didn't crush her.

"Do you still trust me?" he murmured against her lips.

She nodded as she closed her eyes and tipped her head, silently seeking more. But he needed to hear the words.

"Say it," he demanded.

Her eyes met his as her lids fluttered open. "I trust you, Sam. I always have."

"I will make this right for you," he assured her. "And for your brother."

"I know you will. You already have."

"I haven't done enough," he countered. "Not yet."

She started to say something else, but Sam eased back and gripped the hem of her shirt. He hesitated, waiting for any indication that she wasn't ready, but since she'd just agreed to move in with him, he had to assume she was on the same page.

"Do it," she told him.

Being demanding in the bedroom was the sexiest damn thing. Maty had always been bold, assertive. It was one of the main things that had attracted him so long ago and his response now was absolutely no different.

She might have gotten knocked down, but he knew Maty. She would rise from the ashes and be stronger than ever. Sam intended to be right there beside her.

That instant thought scared the hell out of him.

He had no clue where it had come from so he jerked the shirt up and over her head. Sex he understood, but all of the other deeper emotions that kept resurfacing he had no clue what to do with.

Once she was down to only her lacy panties, Sam stood and stripped down. When her eyes raked over him, he pulled in a deep breath. How could his ego not swell when she looked at him as if he were absolutely everything?

"Are you going to stand there all day or are you going to do something about this ache?" she asked.

Sam weighed his options and reached down to jerk the sheet away. Then he hooked his thumbs in the lace on her hips and pulled her panties down her legs and tossed the garment over his shoulder.

"I believe you already had a head start earlier," he told her. "Were you dreaming about anyone in particular?"

Maty's face flushed and he couldn't resist the mix of adorable and sultry. Lying bare in his rumpled bed was a fantasy he hadn't even realized he'd left lingering in his mind. Having her back was both perfect and terrifying. No matter how much he allowed himself to enjoy her body, he couldn't forget that she had left him before. This time, though, he had no preconceived notions about any happily-ever-afters or promises. There was only here and now.

"You expect me to go solo?" she asked, quirking a brow. "I can do that at my apartment."

Sam climbed onto the bed and straddled her, bracing his hands on either side of her head. "You're not going back there," he told her. "The place was a dump when I lived there and it's even worse now."

Maty stared up at him. Her fingertips trailed up his arms and over his shoulders until she threaded her fingers through his hair. He didn't want to control her, but he did want her safe. If he had to be stubborn about it, he would.

"I'm sorry about all of this," she told him.

Rage bubbled within him that Rusty had put her in a position of impossible circumstances and yet she still felt the need to apologize.

"None of this is your fault," he insisted. "But I don't want anything outside of this room to come in here. Right now, there's only us. Problems don't exist."

A smile spread across her face as she eased her legs wider, allowing him to settle even more between her thighs.

"Your world isn't as realistic as mine," she told him. "Money can solve your problems."

"Then we'll use all of my money to solve yours. We can discuss that later."

She started to open her mouth, no doubt to argue, which was clearly an occupational hazard as a lawyer, but he covered her lips with his. Sam didn't want to bicker. He didn't want her to worry about a single thing except feeling each other.

Maty arched against him as her knees came up on either side of his hips. The warmth of her body welcomed him in and he didn't recall another woman who'd ever made him feel this content, this wanted. She'd always been special, always been his.

His?

No.

She wasn't his. He had too much going on. She

could be his physically, but emotionally…never again.

"Protection," she murmured against his mouth. "I'm on birth control, but I don't have anything else."

Oh, he had it, but he didn't want to use it with her if he didn't have to.

"I don't want a barrier," he told her, kissing his way along her jaw and down her neck. "I'm clean and I've always used protection."

He eased back slightly to see her face, to try to gauge what she was feeling, thinking.

"I trust you," he told her.

She framed his face, raking her thumb over his bottom lip. "I haven't been with a man in nearly two years. I'm clean."

Maybe he shouldn't be so thrilled at the fact she'd been alone, but he couldn't deny that he was happy to know she hadn't been with someone in a long time. He wanted all of her to be all of his…but he couldn't keep allowing his thoughts to get too wrapped up in feelings. If he continued to do that, then he would become too emotionally involved.

Sam reached down and gripped her inner thighs, spreading her farther apart. Maty's hips slowly tilted toward him, her eyes never leaving his.

Easing one finger over her heat, Sam continued to watch her. Nothing was sexier than Maty when she was aroused, so he slid into her and worked her with his hand. He shifted on the bed, making sure she knew exactly who was in charge here…though it wouldn't take much for the roles to be reversed.

With his free hand, Sam reached up and slid his palm over her abdomen and up to her breast. Her nipple pebbled beneath his touch and his body responded. Gritting his teeth, he willed himself to take his time. As much as he wanted to join their bodies, he also knew she deserved everything he could give.

Sex wasn't the answer to everything, but it sure as hell would take their minds off things for a while and it felt damn good.

"Sam, please."

Her plea was like gasoline on the fire. His body responded and he wasn't sure how much longer he could deny them both and draw this out.

"Tell me what you want," he demanded.

She reached her hands toward him. "You. Please."

That was all he needed to hear.

Sam came up onto his knees and gripped the back of her thighs. Her hands fell back beside her head, giving her a completely submissive look as she lay ready and willing for him.

The second he joined their bodies, Maty cried out and gripped the pillow in her hands. Sam kept hold of her legs as he started to move. Watching her back arch, her eyes close, her mouth open in ecstasy nearly drove him over the edge.

Maty locked her legs behind his back as she jerked her hips faster against his. Her cries and pants filled the room until her entire body convulsed around him, her knees tightening against his hips as her pleasure overcame her.

Sam wanted to watch her, he wanted to make this last, but he couldn't hold on another second. He followed her release and let the climax consume him.

Maty eased up onto her elbows and watched him, her eyes locking with his. There was something he couldn't identify in her expression, something that he hadn't seen before.

As his trembling slowed, Sam leaned down and covered her mouth with his. He released her legs and slid his hands over hers on the pillow, lacing their fingers together.

He didn't want this moment to end, didn't want her to ever leave his bed…and maybe his life.

That was something he'd have to work out on his own because he wasn't professing anything to her, not when both of their lives were so unstable. He'd been hurt by her once before, and while he planned on keeping her safe and secure, he also wasn't letting his guard down again.

Twelve

Maty stood in the library and pulled in a deep breath as she stared out at the pond. With her cell in one hand, she clutched a glass of wine in the other. She didn't necessarily believe in liquid courage, but having something else to focus on other than this phone call was imperative.

Sam had left for the distillery, to finalize plans for the gala. She honestly had no clue what she was going to wear, but that was another worry for another time.

She gripped the phone and waited. Rusty rarely answered her calls on the first try. She always had to keep calling or she had to leave a message and wait. For someone so hell-bent on buying out his rival, one would think he would answer every single time she called.

Everything with that infuriating man was a mind game.

As usual, Maty got his voice mail and yet again she left a message. Frustrated, she ended the call and took a sip of her Pinot. She couldn't just sit around Sam's house all day and drink wine and play on her phone. She had to be proactive and search for another job.

But where?

The pressure wasn't as strong now that her brother's care was paid for. She had time to figure out if she should go back to Virginia or stay in Tennessee.

Her brother was in Virginia and she didn't want to be too far from him. Sam was in Green Valley.

She couldn't just restructure her life because last night had blown her mind. She couldn't send out résumés in this area simply because sex with Sam was even more powerful and intense than ever before. Good grief, how ridiculous could she be?

Anything deeper than sex that they'd had was in the past. All of this happening between them now was just… Well, she didn't know what label to use.

She knew she wanted to be here, she knew she wanted more of what they'd shared yesterday, but she had so many fears. What if Sam completely took over—as he was so good at doing—and she lost control of her life? She wanted to stand on her own, even though right now, she valued his help. She just didn't want him thinking he could dictate everything for her from now on.

And what if Sam was using her only as a way to pass the time? What if he was using her as more leverage against Rusty?

She had said she didn't like being a pawn in Rusty's game, but she didn't want to be a pawn for anyone. As much as she loved being with Sam again, she wouldn't be some intricate piece in his ploy, either.

Her cell vibrated in her hand and she glanced down to the text on the screen.

Marly and Natalie are coming at one for options for the gala. They work for me. Don't ask prices. Pick out anything you want.

He was sending people here? Like her own personal shoppers? Who did that? She was more than capable of going out to shop on her own. Granted her funds were extremely limited until she found a new job, but she didn't want Sam to completely take over her life now that she'd moved in. That's not why she'd agreed and she had to make sure he understood that. She couldn't have him hovering over her or making all of her decisions.

Maty hit Reply.

We need to talk about all of this taking over you're doing.

She hit Send and reread the message. Did that sound ungrateful? She just didn't know what to do or how to react to this. She certainly wasn't used to someone else caring for her and making decisions. She knew he cared…he had to, right? He wasn't going through all of this with her just for sex.

Maty shook her head and turned from the calming view—which wasn't calming her at all—and glanced at the wall of books. A book didn't interest her right now, so she glanced to the desk and spotted a notepad. Yes, that's what she needed to relax her because her paranoia was taking over. She'd doodle and draw a bit.

As she settled into the oversize leather desk chair, her cell vibrated again, but not with a text. Rusty's name lit up the screen.

She took another sip of her wine, settled her glass beside the notepad and answered.

"Rusty," she greeted with a smile hoping the fake gesture came through in her tone. "Thanks for returning my call."

"I assume you have news for me."

She hated his smug tone; it always made her feel like he was on some other level and she was far beneath him.

It would be a pleasure to help Sam bring him down. Men like Rusty Lockwood had no respect for other people.

"I think I have Sam almost ready to commit."

"I knew I just had to tighten the reins," he scoffed.

Maty had to grit her teeth and take a reassuring breath to not verbally explode all over the bastard. Playing with her brother's health was not a way to get on her good side and now that she could fight back, she was coming up with both fists swinging.

All of this gave her renewed hope that she was finally positioned toward the right direction in this new chapter of her life. Not that she purposefully wanted to be deceitful, but these were circumstances she'd never expected and she had to make the best of an impossible situation. At least with Sam knowing the truth, Maty had more control over her life than she'd had just yesterday.

"It will require more money," she told him, immediately thinking up the lie on the fly. "An extra ten million on top of the offer you already extended."

"Ten million? That's ridiculous."

Maty smiled and swirled the contents of her glass. "That's the price he said, so if you want this as bad as you say you do, I would agree."

Or maybe he had to use his extra funds to pay

off his other attorneys for the cheating he had been doing with the Milestones charity. Oh, the tangled web he was weaving...

"See if you can get him to come down," Rusty finally replied.

"So when you said any amount, you didn't really mean it," she retorted. "If money is a problem—"

"I don't have financial problems," he growled. "I'm Rusty Lockwood, damn it."

Oh, that sounded like he had a multitude of problems *because* he was Rusty Lockwood. Perhaps this dynasty he'd started illegally forty years ago was starting to crumble. Maybe he knew he was about to lose what he'd worked for. A scandal the magnitude of one around stealing from a children's charity would certainly be damning to a company that prided itself on donations and with a reputation of encouraging its employees to contribute as well.

Maty had no sympathy for this monster. He'd sought her out during her most vulnerable time and forced her to face her past. Granted she didn't mind being reunited with Sam, but the stakes were too great. Her heart was on the line now and all she had left was her reputation...something she wouldn't let Rusty Lockwood tarnish.

"Then agree to this arrangement and I'll get the legal forms started," she told him, pouring out all the confidence and BS she could muster. "We can wrap this up in a couple of weeks and Hawkins Distillery will be all yours."

Silence again. She hated the quiet almost as much as she hated his smugness. All of that dead air made her twitchy because she knew he was thinking... calculating. There was nothing more dangerous than a maniac who had time to plot.

Maty had faith in Sam, though. He wouldn't be swindled or deceived and he was always working ahead, formulating the perfect approach.

"Fine. Ten million on top of the original offer and I want this done by the end of next week."

What a jerk. Little did he know...

"Fine," she agreed. "But next time I call, you'll need to answer. I don't have time for phone tag."

Rusty chuckled. "I'm a busy man, Ms. Taylor. I'll answer when I'm ready."

With that, he hung up and it took everything in her not to throw her phone across the room. Instead, she tossed back the remaining wine and cursed under her breath.

"Arrogant bastard."

"I couldn't agree more."

Startled, Maty jerked her head up to see Sam leaning against the door frame. His width consumed nearly the entire opening and that dark gaze held her in place. Her heart beat a heavy rhythm and she wasn't sure if it was from being startled because she'd thought she was alone or from the sexy man only a few feet away.

"I thought you were at the distillery."

Maty tried to be calm as she set her empty glass on the desk and pocketed her phone. After last night, she hadn't seen much of him. He'd gotten up, kissed her forehead and told her he'd see her later. He'd suggested she make his home like hers. Easier said than done when she was a nervous wreck.

Sex changed everything. Great sex changed every thought and was slowly working on her heart. So she hadn't been able to relax in his home. Couple that with the call to Rusty and she needed that wineglass refilled.

"I'm quick when it comes to decision making," he told her with a half grin. "And my assistant had already chosen most things considering he knows me better than nearly anyone."

At one time that honor had belonged to her, but she'd thrown away their bond for her future. Look how well those dreams had turned out. She'd wanted something of her own, something she could be proud of. What would she have done had she stayed behind?

That was all in the past and she couldn't change the decisions she'd made years ago.

She could, however, decide what type of future she was going to have. Regaining control was a step in the right direction. She just had to watch that next step so she didn't end up with a heartache.

"I take it from the drained glass of wine and your muttering a moment ago that the call didn't go well?"

Maty shrugged. "I talked him into ten million more than the original number."

Sam stared at her for a moment before he busted out laughing and crossed the room. "We didn't discuss that."

"No, we didn't. I sort of made it up as I went along."

He came to stand directly in front of the desk and her heart quickened once again. That seemed to be the norm lately whenever Sam got near. Even with the past they shared, this was simply an entirely new dynamic. They had both been young before and had assumed love could carry them through anything.

Now, well, they were older and more experienced—and more cautious.

He glanced down to the empty wineglass and the notebook. "Trying to relax?" he asked.

Maty shrugged. "Nothing's working."

Sam circled the desk and came to stand before her. When he reached his hands out, she took hold and came to her feet.

Trailing those rough fingertips up her arms, Sam and his simple, innocent touch caused a curl of arousal to spiral through her. She continued to stare up into those dark, heavy-lidded eyes.

"Remind me not to get on your bad side," he told her, gripping her shoulders and offering a sultry smile. "You're quite impressive. I might be looking for an attorney to add to my team."

Maty stilled. "Excuse me?"

"Would you want to work for me? No blackmailing," he quickly added. "I'm not saying this because I'm sleeping with you, either. I expect the best from my employees and they have to be honest and loyal."

She wanted to reach up, to rake over that stubble along his jaw and feel it on her palm. She wanted to feel that connection, the way they had last night.

But she also had to remain strong and keep her common sense in front of her heart for protection. Just because he was intrigued by her professional skills and they were more than compatible in the sheets, didn't mean everything would be shiny and perfect in a working atmosphere. A job with his company would be long-term and a leap she wasn't ready to take.

"I can't jump right into working for you," she explained.

His brows drew in. "Why not?"

"Because... Well... I just can't."

He smirked. "Not a very good defense. Try again."

Maty pulled away and turned toward the windows. She took a few steps, just to put a bit more distance between them so she could gather her thoughts. Her gaze landed in the distance at the pond and the mountains surrounding the property. She wondered what this would look like in the fall, imagining all the vibrant colors, and if she'd be around to see the beauty.

"I may be in Virginia," she murmured, still staring out the window. "I'm not sure I'll stay here."

Silence crackled in the air and she glanced over her shoulder to gauge his reaction.

"I guess I shouldn't have assumed you'd stay."

There was a tone in his voice she couldn't quite name. Part of her wondered if he'd be hurt if she left, but neither had promised each other anything.

Maty turned fully to face him. "I don't know what I'm doing," she admitted. "I want to be near my brother. He's all the family I have left. At the same time, what if I'm meant to be somewhere else? I mean, I know you graciously paid for Carter's care, but at some point I need to take over. I need my own insurance and I need to make my own life and start over."

"Who says you can't start over in Green Valley?" he asked.

Maty studied his expression, not sure if she actually saw more than lust, more than revenge. There were so many emotions that made up this Sam as opposed to the Sam of sixteen years ago. She and

Sam had both been through quite a few changes, yet here they were right back together, still unable to deny their attraction.

"I can't make a life-altering decision right now," she told him honestly. "Can I just…can I stay here with you until…"

Sam took a step, then another, until he closed the distance between them. He framed her face and tipped her head back as he towered over her.

"You can stay here as long as you want," he murmured, leaning down to graze his lips across hers. "I won't be the one to make you leave."

That statement held so much power, and put the decision solely on her…just like the first time. So much had changed, yet so much had remained the same.

Maty would stay until everything with Rusty was resolved and after that…

Yeah, it was the *after that* that terrified her because she wanted so much, but she dared not hope and risk a broken heart again.

Thirteen

Sam stared at the glass decanter that he'd designed himself. Well, he hadn't exactly come up with the design, but only one other person would know that.

He couldn't believe the day of his first official bourbon release was actually approaching. First, the gala to really hype up his high-end clientele and then in just a few short months, the first distribution would take place around the world. In five more years, he'd unveil his fifteen-year bourbon, five more would be his twenty. There was a cycle he was starting and he couldn't wait to see what the future held.

The warehouses were stocked with barrels that

were rolled on a very strict schedule. Sometimes he'd walk through those pathways between the stacks to take in the aroma of charred wood and bourbon. There was really nothing like that scent. Sam couldn't believe this was his life now and he never took for granted a single day or all the possibilities of things to come.

His professional life—he had a strong, firm handle on. It was the personal aspect that had gotten so far out of control, he had no idea which part to fix first.

His mother was going to finally get the help she needed, the clock was ticking on Rusty's little game monopolizing the hard liquor industry, and Maty...

Hell, he had no clue.

If he were being honest with himself, he wanted more. Maybe that was the past talking, maybe that was this new phase they'd entered. Who knew?

He did know that now that he and Maty had stripped each other and had fast, frantic sex in the main warehouse, he'd never be able to walk through there again without getting somewhat aroused.

He couldn't wait to take her to the gala. He wondered if she'd know the significance behind the shape of the bottle. Would she even remember? Was he a complete fool for using the design she'd drawn for him so long ago?

Maybe, but this was his company and he'd damn well do what he wanted. Besides, this design had been his favorite option and the only one he'd actually considered.

Sam placed the glass bottle back in his office safe and secured the door with the code. The familiar ring from his cell chimed from his desk.

He crossed his office and grabbed the phone from a pile of brochures from potential distributors he'd been researching. Nick's name flashed on the screen and Sam welcomed the distraction from his thoughts.

"Hey, man. What's up?" he answered.

"I don't have much time because Silvia is making me choose different lighting for the bathrooms at the resort. Don't ask. That's a whole ordeal I don't want to get into."

Sam laughed. "Okay. So why did you call if you're swamped?"

"Because I just heard that the city council called a special meeting for Friday afternoon."

Sam stilled. "I assume this is about the liquor license or you wouldn't be postponing your lighting date with your wife."

"Such a smart-ass," Nick muttered. "We have to be related."

Sam couldn't help but smile. He had a half brother. This was beyond anything he ever could've imagined. Sam wanted to know all the details of their pasts and how they now intertwined. He also wanted to know who their other brother was.

So many other factors were taking precedence right now, though.

"Yes, to answer your question," Nick went on. "It is about the licensing. Nobody knows this meeting is taking place, but I have an inside guy."

"And you don't think Lockwood knows what's going on? Isn't he the one with all these guys in his pockets?"

Sam had to play the devil's advocate. He had to cover all his bases in order to stay a step ahead of the game. But his point was quite valid. All of this was an utter mess because decades ago, when Rusty started illegally making and selling moonshine discreetly, he became part of the good ol' boys' club where council members overlooked some of Rusty's dealings in exchange for white lightning.

So when moonshine became legal not too long ago, Rusty already had an in and secured his hard liquor license, and the council wrote the laws for the county that made moonshine the only hard liquor to be sold in restaurants.

"I trust this person completely and I truly believe Rusty will have no clue," Nick replied. "Apparently you and I have intrigued some of Rusty's cronies, and the facts we've presented coupled with the resort and your new bourbon reveal is enough to get them thinking on the right path. Listen, I know you have the gala that night, but I wanted to give you a heads-up in case something happens and Rusty decides to cause a problem."

Sam gripped his cell and sneered. "I dare him to try to cross me. He won't like the outcome."

"Oh, he won't like the outcome of this meeting, I'm sure," Nick stated with a chuckle. "Hopefully with both of us at the gala, he won't be dumb enough to make a move in front of so many heavy hitters in the industry."

Everyone from politicians to restaurateurs to billion-dollar CEOs was invited and expected to attend. Who didn't want to be part of this new endeavor? The hype around a new bourbon was huge, but add in Sam being the youngest master distiller in the country and the media was having a feeding frenzy. Sam sure as hell didn't want Rusty or any other scandal to tarnish what promised to be a perfect night.

"I need to go," Nick told him. "Apparently she's found the lights she wants. I'll see you Friday."

Sam disconnected the call and was about to shove the cell in his pocket when it chimed again with a text from his mother.

Can you come by later?

He shot back a quick text.

Sure thing.

Glancing at the time, he knew he could go ahead and leave. All of the reports were done, he'd done a couple of employee reviews and he'd managed to confirm all parties involved in going to his house on Friday to help Maty get ready for the gala for her hair and makeup. Not that it mattered what she wore or what she did with her hair. The woman was shockingly stunning and stole his breath every time they were together.

But he couldn't wait to have her by his side. Maybe it was all egotistical, but Sam wanted her to be proud of all he'd accomplished. When they'd been together before, that's all he'd wanted. Impressing her had been paramount because at the time he'd felt so unworthy. She was a rich girl from a prominent family. They'd welcomed him from the start, but he'd always felt like he didn't belong in their big fancy house with matching silverware and dinner parties.

Now, though, he realized that her family had been good people. They truly hadn't cared about his background or his financial status. They were supportive of his wild ideas to one day own his own distillery. They could've laughed or blown it off, considering he had no money, but they'd entertained his thoughts. Sam still couldn't believe they were gone. He hated that Maty had lost them, that she was dealing with her brother's paralysis and this mess with Rusty. She'd been handling too much on her own and Sam wasn't going to let her carry the load alone any longer.

He would do everything he could to get her back on her feet, to make her feel better about this new chapter she had to start without her parents. Sam wanted the best for her, but he didn't know what that was…only she could decide that.

Part of him wanted her to decide to stay in Green Valley for good, but the other part was terrified she'd do just that. If she stayed in Green Valley, then what? Would they try for a real relationship again? Was life really that easy?

Maybe, maybe not.

He was a fool for even allowing his thoughts to wander down the path that led to some silly happily-ever-after. Maty had admitted that she wasn't sure Green Valley was for her, so he might as well just enjoy the hell out of her while she's here and keep his heart and emotions out of the equation. Hadn't he learned his lesson the first time around?

Sam took the back way out of the office and headed to his truck. He didn't typically have anxiety, but between this reunion with Maty and the Rusty situation possibly coming to a close soon, how could he not be on edge?

He cranked up the music and took the windy back roads to his mom's house. He needed those extra few minutes to clear his head. He knew he needed to maintain some sort of emotional distance from

Maty, but that was proving to be more and more difficult. He couldn't just shut off his emotions. No matter how much he'd dodged relationships for all these years, that didn't mean he was cold or unfeeling.

He wasn't going to try to pretend he wouldn't hurt if she left. Maty had always had a hold over him that he'd never been able to explain.

Sam couldn't help but wonder what, if any, hold he had over her.

When he pulled into his mother's drive, she stepped out onto the cottage porch and smiled. She looked more tired than ever, but she was still a beautiful woman. She'd worked herself hard her entire life, sometimes making poor decisions, but she loved him with her entire being.

She'd put aside that money from Rusty when he'd paid her off. If she hadn't cared about Sam, if she'd been that selfish, she never would have thought of her unborn baby's future.

Sam loved her just as much. He wanted to see her well. He wanted her to get the help she needed, the help she had finally agreed to get. He wanted her to come out on the other side with a renewed hope for her future and a fresh start.

Just like Maty was doing.

Damn it. Every thought lately circled back to her. He wouldn't mind if he could pinpoint what the hell they had going on. Sex would take them only so far and it was a hell of a ride while it lasted, but then what?

Ignoring the impending thoughts of an end he didn't want to experience again, Sam stepped from his truck and headed up the stone sidewalk.

"You didn't have to leave work early," his mother told him as he mounted the steps.

Sam bent down to kiss her cheek and smiled. "I'm the CEO. I have nobody to answer to except my mother."

She rolled her eyes and swatted him, but her playful mood quickly sobered.

"I just wanted you to know the facility called and they can take me in on Friday morning instead of Monday."

Friday morning. Which meant she wouldn't be there to see his gala, to see the unveiling of the bourbon and to share that monumental moment with him.

Her health came first, though. Above all else, he wanted her to get to the sanctuary that would heal her.

"That's great news," he told her.

Her lips pursed as she folded her arms over her small frame. "I want to postpone it until next week."

"No," he insisted. "You're going. Don't worry about the gala. I have years and years of bourbons coming out. I'll save you a bottle from the first batch."

"I hope to be out before you launch in the fall."

She laughed, then patted his cheek. "I just wanted to be by your side for your big night."

Sam took her shoulders and pulled her into a hug. "I know you did and that's all that matters. But, for me, I need my mother to get well and heal."

Her arms came around his waist as she laid her head against his chest. "I knew you'd say that," she murmured.

Sam eased back and glanced down. "Then why are we having this conversation?"

"I was hoping you'd convince the facility to let me come in on Saturday morning instead."

One day. She was asking for only one day because she wanted to show her support for him.

"Please."

Sam kissed her forehead and nodded. "I'll call them today."

For what he'd paid and the strings he'd pulled to get her into the place, he had no doubt they'd accommodate her arriving later.

"I have to tell you that there may be an issue with Rusty," he told her, but cut her off when she opened her mouth. "It's nothing I can't handle. I'm just giving you a heads-up. This is all business. He has no clue I'm his son and I'd like to keep it that way for as long as possible."

Nick had opted to tell the old bastard, but Sam wanted to keep that truth bottled up until this ordeal with the liquor licenses was settled. He wanted the local liquor industry to be opened up, where Rusty wasn't the sole provider to the resorts and restaurants in this growing area. Once Rusty had lost some of his momentum and clout, Sam wouldn't mind telling him the truth at all. There would be no grand father/son bonding time, he was sure, which was just fine with him, but he did wonder how the old man would react.

Thankfully, by that time his mother would be in her facility and away from Rusty's influence. Sam didn't want that man anywhere near the people he cared about…hence having Maty move in with him.

"Don't mess with him any more than you have to," she told him. "I mean it, Sam. He's evil."

"He is," Sam agreed. "But I'm smarter and I have more power. I'm not afraid of him."

"I just don't want to worry about you while I'm gone."

Sam stepped back and smiled. "Then don't. I promise to visit and call and check on you often. You'll know exactly what's going on."

Her eyes welled with tears and he swiped the moisture from her dark skin. "I'm so sorry I'm doing this to you," she said. "You have so much to worry about without always rushing to help me."

"I have nothing else to do if you're not well," he countered. "So, are you ready for the gala? You have the dress and shoes? I have a stylist coming to do your hair and makeup."

Good thing he had a handy assistant who could make all of this happen for his mother and Maty. He just wanted the two women in his life to have a perfect night and he didn't want either of them to worry about a thing.

She laughed. "I can do my own hair and makeup."

"Maybe I want to pamper you." His cell vibrated in his pocket, but he ignored it. "Just plan on being available from about ten that morning until I send a car to pick you up."

She smiled and reached up to pat the side of his face. "I'm really proud of you. I just want you to always know that. I don't know what would happen to me if it weren't for you."

Sam tamped down his emotions. He needed to be strong for her. She'd cared for him so long and now it was his turn to make sure she found a way back to taking care of herself.

"I know you struggle with this addiction, but we're going to make it better."

He pulled her into an embrace once more, hoping to prove to her how much he loved her, to reassure her he would always be here no matter what.

Rusty wouldn't get near her or anyone else Sam cared for. He would do anything to stop that man from any more destruction.

Fourteen

Maty stared at her reflection in the floor-length mirror. She turned side to side and wondered if she'd made a mistake. Maybe she should've gone with the red dress instead. Something that made a statement instead of being boring and predictable.

"You're not going anywhere in that."

Maty glanced over her shoulder in the mirror and saw Sam standing a few feet behind her. He wore a white button-up shirt with the top two buttons undone, a black jacket and black dress pants. He'd even groomed his hair for the occasion, but that jaw scruff was still prominent and so damn sexy. A little rough and a little class all rolled into one mouth-watering package.

He was all hers…at least for now.

But it was that dark, heavy gaze that raked over her twice that confirmed she had indeed chosen the perfect dress.

Her stomach knotted with arousal and anticipation for the night to come. She had no idea what to expect, but she knew there would be something phenomenal.

"Damn." Sam took a step toward her. "Remind me to give my assistant a raise and that stylist an extra tip. I really should keep you home all to myself."

"You can't miss your own gala," she told him.

He curled his fingers around her biceps and pulled her back against his chest. Their stares met in the mirror. Feeling his warmth combined with those eyes that continually captivated her had her wanting to ditch the very public event, too.

"Maybe we could be extremely late," he suggested, grazing his lips along the sensitive spot between her neck and her shoulder.

His hands slid around her waist and covered her abdomen. Maty tipped her head to the side and laced her fingers through his.

"I think we should just go now before we get to a point we can't leave," she suggested. "Think of it as foreplay and when we come back tonight…

maybe I'll let you see what I'm not wearing beneath this dress."

Sam groaned and spun her around. Maty yelped as she caught herself and grabbed hold of his shoulders. His mouth came within a breath of hers.

"Don't tease me," he growled. "I didn't know I'd come in and see you looking like sex wrapped in silk."

Maty loved knowing she could affect him so strongly. Whatever was developing between them was more intense than she'd ever expected. When she'd been forced to come back to Green Valley, she'd truly had no idea what to expect with Sam. She wasn't sorry she came back; she just didn't like the circumstances regarding her return.

But she couldn't be sorry about any of it now. Even though she hated Rusty for putting her in an impossible situation, this path had led her back into Sam's arms. She wondered if she would stay there.

Maty toyed with the top button of his dress shirt. "Maybe if you're good, I'll let you unwrap me later."

He started to lean in, but she skirted around him. As much as she wanted his mouth and hands on her, she couldn't let that get started. Once he touched her in any sort of intimate way, she knew this dress would be off and her hair would be a disaster.

"I'm all set to go," she told him, swiping her delicate gold clutch from the vanity.

Sam crossed to her and slid his hand over the

curve of her hip and leaned in. "There's no one else I'd want by my side tonight. This means more than anything."

His words sank in as he escorted her out with his hand on the small of her back. She'd expected him to say something else sexual or maybe even trail those lips along the side of her neck to drive her wild.

But he'd been sincere with his words, giving her a glimpse of that heart of his. Maybe there was a future for them. Maybe she could stay here and build her new life. She wasn't that far from Virginia.

Is that what she wanted to do? Did she want to start this whole new chapter of her life back where she'd begun? Was she ready to risk her heart, her future, on one man in the hopes that he could love her back?

Love her back.

Maty stopped in the foyer as the realization slammed into her.

"You okay?" Sam asked as he glanced to her.

She wanted to tell him, to be completely open and honest with her feelings. This sudden burst of happiness consumed her, but now was not the time. He had the most important night of his career just ahead and she wanted him to be solely focused on the dream he'd worked so hard for.

What if he didn't feel the same as she did? Then she'd put those words out there and the evening would turn awkward and uncomfortable.

Maty smiled and turned to face him. She framed his face and briefly touched her lips to his.

"I'm great," she told him. "But when we get back, I have something to tell you."

His eyes widened. "Are you pregnant?"

Maty laughed. "No, but good to know that would freak you out."

He blinked and shook his head. "I actually want a family someday, I just… Damn it, you threw me there. Do you want to tell me what's on your mind now?"

Maty reached for his hand and laced their fingers together. "When we get back."

"Is that before or after I unwrap you?" he asked with a sultry grin.

"Depends on if you can wait that long to unwrap me," she replied with a wink. "Now let's get to your gala. You can't keep your guests waiting."

Samples of Hawkins ten-year bourbon flowed amongst the guests. The very first barrel ever used sat on display in the middle of the main lobby area. A framed letter sat atop the barrel explaining Sam's journey to this moment.

He glanced around at the mingling guests and couldn't help the swell of pride that overcame him. This was what he'd been waiting for his whole life. That sense of accomplishment, that sense of worth.

But something was missing. He'd thought this

night would bring a feeling of wholeness that he'd been lacking, but there was still a void he couldn't put his finger on.

He caught his mother's gaze from across the room where she had been chatting with a restaurateur from Miami. She looked positively beautiful in her simple blue gown. When she smiled at him, he knew they were going to be alright, *she* was going to be alright.

"Mr. Hawkins."

Sam turned toward the boisterous tone and smiled as the governor approached with his hand extended.

"Great turnout," Governor Pate said, pumping Sam's hand. "Great bourbon, too."

"Glad you're enjoying yourself, Governor."

"I'd like to purchase a barrel for my inauguration," he went on.

"Expecting another win?" Sam asked with a grin.

"I didn't go into this expecting to lose." He laughed. "I'll have my assistant get in touch with yours next week. This is by far the best bourbon I've ever had."

Sam nodded. "I'll be sure to let my assistant know to expect a call."

His eyes roamed over the governor's shoulder and landed on Maty. Her back was to him—her back with that damn low-cut dress that exposed too much skin. Where black fabric did cover her, the satin hugged every damn curve.

Sam returned his attention to his guest. "If you'll excuse me," he said.

The governor turned and zeroed in on Maty. "Of course. You're a lucky man."

Sam smiled and nodded in agreement as he stepped away.

This was it. This was what had been missing in his life. Maty Taylor. Had she always been the one for him? Obviously so, but it had taken years apart and her stepping back at the most vulnerable time for both of them. Maybe that's the only way they could heal and grow together once again? Maybe this was the moment in time when they were supposed to be together and sixteen years ago had just been all wrong.

Everything was right now.

As he walked to her, he spotted Nick and Silvia across the room. Nick's arm slid around his wife's waist and he pulled her to his side in that protective way Sam totally understood.

He hadn't had a chance to speak to his brother, yet… Sam loved thinking of Nick in that way. To Sam's knowledge, Nick hadn't heard a word about the private council meeting that supposedly took place this afternoon. Sam couldn't worry about that right now, but he would be looking into it as soon as this gala was over…and after he delivered on his promise to Maty of their own private celebration.

While he couldn't wait to get back home with

her, he also knew she had something she wanted to tell him. That split second when a baby popped into his mind had scared him, but after a moment he sort of liked the idea of her carrying his baby. There would be nobody else in the world he'd want to have a family with.

But he had to tell her the truth. All of it. About Rusty, about Nick. Would Lockwood being Sam's father be a complete turnoff for her? Would she not want to associate with Sam after what Rusty had done to her? Would she feel threatened because the man had attempted to ruin her career and her life?

The fear was extremely real.

Sam was approached multiple times before he could make it across the room to Maty. By the time he'd extracted himself from all of the congrats and handshakes, Maty was gone.

He turned again and found her up on the second floor where the wraparound balcony overlooked the main area. She was standing next to his mother and Maty's hand was on his mom's arm as the two smiled at each other.

Sam's heart swelled and filled with such emotions, he couldn't even describe the collision of them all. His past stood right in front of him…his future, too.

Moving to the one set of steps that led to the second floor, Sam nodded in greeting to several guests as he passed through. He couldn't wait until he unveiled the bottle design in the next hour. Anxiety bubbled within because he had no idea if Maty would remember or if she'd even care that he'd taken her drawing from when they'd dated.

He hoped she remembered. He hoped this was just another puzzle piece in merging their lives back together.

"Sam."

He turned just as he'd gotten to the bottom of the steps. Nick and Silvia approached him and Sam moved over to clear the path for other guests mingling.

"Sorry I haven't been around to see you guys, yet," Sam stated. "I appreciate you all being here."

"We wouldn't be anywhere else," Nick told him as held up his tumbler. "This stuff is amazing, man. Seriously. I can't wait to have it in my resort."

Sam stilled. "What?"

Nick smiled, but Silvia chimed in. "We wanted to tell you in person that the council has overturned the law and Rusty is no longer top dog."

As if Sam's night could get any better. He glanced to Nick.

"Are you positive?" he asked.

Nick nodded. "I got a call from my source just before coming here."

Elated and more than intrigued, Sam crossed his arms and shifted so his back was to the crowd, to give them a little privacy.

"I have to know, who is this source?" he murmured.

"Councilman Perry's son." Nick chuckled. "I buddied up with him a few weeks ago when I learned he had moved back to the area. I offered him the position of resort manager and a lot of perks. Though John will make an excellent manager, his first job was getting in the room with his dad. I had the right person in our corner who helped make our case."

Sam couldn't believe it. He honestly could not believe what was happening. All of his dreams, new ones and old ones, were coming together to make a path for his future.

"Does Rusty know?" Sam asked.

Nick shrugged and finished his tumbler of bourbon before handing it off to a member of the waitstaff.

"That I'm not sure of," he replied. "If he doesn't now, it won't be long before he does. So we both need to be aware that he will likely retaliate in some way."

"Hopefully he's too busy fighting his other battle with the rumor of him skimming from the charity he endorses."

But knowing Rusty, he wouldn't just go away quietly. Hell, he wouldn't go away with blaring horns and whistles. Someone like Lockwood would never admit defeat.

"Maybe if he finds out he's my father, too, then he'll realize—"

Nick's eyes widened and Silvia's gaze darted over Sam's shoulder. He turned to see his mother and

Maty standing just behind them. He'd been so consumed with his own thoughts, he hadn't even heard them approach.

"Rusty is your father?" Maty whispered as if she couldn't bear to say the words.

He shifted fully to face her. "Maty, I—"

She held up her hands. "No. Just answer my question."

Sam swallowed and glanced to his mother who stared back at him with such sadness and sorrow. He hated that he'd kept this from Maty. He should've told her when he learned the truth about her situation, but at that point he honestly hadn't known if he could trust her.

"He is," Sam confirmed. "And Nick is my half brother."

Maty's wide eyes never moved from him. The noise around them continued as if his entire world hadn't just blown up in his face.

"Let's go into my office and talk."

Sam started to reach for her, but she gathered her dress in one hand and held on to her clutch with the other. She stepped up to him and her eyes narrowed.

"I won't cause a scene here," she muttered between gritted teeth. "But we have nothing to discuss, so I'm leaving."

He'd almost rather she throw a fit, scream at him or cause that scene. The low, quiet tone laced with hurt and regret gutted him.

"Don't go," he pleaded. "Just…stay. I don't have any right to ask, but I'm asking anyway."

She tipped her chin and glared. Oh, now she was pissed combined with the hurt, and that combination was never good.

"I'll find my own ride," she replied before she skirted around him.

Sam turned to see her stride gracefully through the crowd, even pausing to smile at the guests. She wasn't causing a scene. The random onlooker would never know the turmoil that had just surfaced.

Even though he'd lied and hurt her, she still put his needs first, which spoke volumes about this woman he'd fallen in love with. Damn it. He loved her with his entire heart and she was walking out… and he didn't believe she was just leaving the distillery. She was leaving him. Again.

"Go after her."

Sam glanced over his shoulder. "It won't matter, Mom. She's too upset."

"I didn't know," Nick stated. "I'm sorry, man. I didn't even think."

Sam sighed and turned back to his brother. "I'm the one who said something and I'm the one who should've told her to begin with. But the timing was never good and then I just… Damn it."

"Why don't you go to your office and take a minute?" his mom suggested. "We can cover for you and say you're with a potential client."

Sam shook his head. "No. I'm going through with this night. I won't let Rusty take everything from me."

Of course he'd love to blame all of this on Rusty, but everything that had happened in the last five minutes was all on Sam.

Despair like he'd never known before settled deep. What was supposed to be the best night of his life had suddenly turned into the absolute worst, and all of this could have been avoided if he'd only been honest. If he'd only realized sooner that Maty wasn't the enemy.

She was his everything.

Fifteen

She was a damn fool.

Maty stared at her meager bag and refused to let the tears flow. Her life had been reduced to one bag and a heartbreak she didn't know if she'd ever overcome.

She did know one thing—Rusty and Sam deserved each other.

After calling for a driver to come pick her up, she'd come straight to Sam's house to gather her things. There was no use in staying here. She'd just have to get a hotel for the night and head back to Virginia in the morning. She was simply too exhausted to think about driving tonight.

She glanced down to her gown and laughed at the absurdity. She needed to get out of this dress and leave it behind, but she hadn't even given her wardrobe a thought. When she'd come back, her only concern had been to get her things and get out. But she couldn't exactly leave in a dress that didn't belong to her.

Maty pulled in a shaky breath and reached up to slide the thick straps down her shoulders. With the drape front and back, the dress was easy to slip out of.

"Leave it."

Startled, Maty spun around, holding the top against her chest as she pulled the straps back up and met Sam's intense stare.

"What are you doing here?" she asked.

He filled the entire doorway, hands shoved in his pockets, as he continued to hold her gaze.

"You're in my house."

If she wasn't taking off the dress, she could at least take off the jewelry. Maty slid her finger over the clasp of the gold bracelet and unlatched it.

"You left your own gala," she said, stating the obvious.

He lifted a shoulder and stepped into the room. "I stayed long enough to unveil the new bottle. There are enough people there to cover for me should I be needed now. Some things are more important."

He'd left the gala.

The night he'd been planning for months, years. He'd left to come find her.

He hadn't chased her years ago, but he did now.

"I'm getting my stuff and I'll be gone," she informed him. Even though part of her thrilled to the idea that he'd come for her, that gesture didn't excuse the fact that he'd deceived her.

"Do you want to hear my side?" he asked. "You above all people know there are two sides to every story."

Maty took out one earring, then the other. She took off all the jewelry and placed each piece back in the appropriate velvet pouches. She attempted a few calming breaths before turning back around.

"You admitted to Rusty being your father," she reminded him. "That's pretty damning evidence that you were playing me, unless you tell me that Nick told you only moments before I overheard you."

The muscle in his jaw clenched and Maty's heart cracked a little more. She chewed the inside of her cheek, willing the pain to hold off until she could be alone and have herself a glass of wine and a good cry.

Until then, she would shore up every ounce of strength and get through this...just like she had every other soul-crushing blow life had thrown at her.

"I only learned of Rusty being my father a few weeks ago," he told her. "That first time you called, I was in the middle of opening a letter, but your call distracted me."

Maty nodded. As much as she wanted out of here, she deserved an explanation.

"I ended up opening it a little later in the day. Apparently, it had come in the mail while I'd been out of town," he went on. "I discovered that it was Nick's mother who sent the letter. She passed away, but not before having three letters sent out to Rusty's sons."

Maty went to the edge of the bed and wrapped her hand around the post. "Three letters? Nick, you, and who is the third brother?"

Sam shook his head. "We have no idea. Nobody has come forward. Either they don't know, they don't believe the letter from a stranger or they don't care that Rusty Lockwood is their father."

She still couldn't process all of this. The man she'd once loved was the son of the man who'd blackmailed her in a vile, evil way. Is that the type of man Sam had turned into? How could she trust anything he said?

"What did Rusty say when you told him?" she asked.

"I haven't told him," Sam stated. "Nick met with him last month and Rusty knows that connection, but he doesn't know about me."

"Are you afraid to tell him?"

Sam stared at her a moment before raking a hand over his stubbled jaw. "I'm not afraid of him, but I don't want to open that door just yet. As long as I have this secret to myself, then I still have a hold over him."

Maty could understand that. She also figured telling Rusty wouldn't change a thing. The man had no heart and he likely wouldn't care about children. Whatever Sam decided to do had to work for him… because she was no longer in the equation.

"You have to live with your own decisions," she told him. "Every choice has a consequence, some good and some bad."

"Are you referring to Lockwood or yourself?" he asked.

Maty swallowed. "Both."

"I never intended to hurt you."

"But you did."

Hadn't she warned herself this could happen? Hadn't she felt that sinking gut sensation the moment she saw him face-to-face again? How could she love someone and hate them at the same time?

Because she didn't hate Sam. She hated his actions and the heartache, but she could never hate him.

"When you first came to me, you were working for my enemy," he explained. "I had no idea the woman you'd become. For all I knew, you wanted to work for him. I couldn't trust you with the truth."

Well, that declaration hurt, but he had a point. They didn't know how the other had turned out.

Sixteen years was a long chunk of time for person-alities and morals to change.

"So once you got me in your bed and then moved into your house, were you still unable to trust me with the truth?"

Sam took a step forward. She didn't stop him. Maty kept her eyes locked on his, refusing to back down or show that she couldn't handle this situation even though she felt ready to crumble.

"I was going to tell you the truth, Maty." He stopped right in front of her and stared down with those dark, mesmerizing eyes. "I want to build something with you and I wanted to wait until this gala was over, until I saw what was going on with Rusty, to tell you everything."

"That's what I would say, too, if I'd been caught."

"It's the truth," he insisted.

Maty gave his defense some consideration. Even if that had been his plan, the fact of the matter was he hadn't trusted her enough, or their relationship enough, to tell her the truth. After all Rusty had done to her, hadn't she deserved to know what she was dealing with? From the moment Sam realized she was a nonthreat, he should have revealed the truth.

"It may be the truth," she amended. "But that doesn't make your silence all this time any less painful. You had to have known how much this would hurt."

Sam swiped a hand along his jaw, and she heard

the coarse hair bristle against his palm. "I thought any time I told you that it would look bad, that you'd be hurt. I wanted to get to know the real you again, to make sure I could trust you. And then, things escalated and I was so focused on you and my mother…"

His voice broke on that last word and a piece of Maty's heart broke right along with it. No matter what his intentions were, he still had to own up to his actions.

She came to her feet, but he didn't step back. Her chest brushed against his and she had to steel herself against all of those instant emotions and needs. Now was not the time for sex. Intimacy wouldn't solve her problems.

"I need to get out of this dress," she told him. "And I need to leave."

He stared at her another minute and she wished he'd move because she couldn't stand this close and remember the promises they'd made to each other for tonight.

A bubble of emotion welled up in her throat. She was supposed to be professing her love to him, letting him know she wanted to try this again. Instead, they were standing here utterly broken and holding on to very little hope.

"You can keep the dress," he told her, his tone husky.

"No, I can't."

He nodded and took a step back. "Then change and come to my den. Please."

She didn't answer right away, in fact it was on the tip of her tongue to tell him no, but in the end she nodded her agreement.

Sam turned and left her alone in his bedroom. Maty blew out a breath she didn't even know she'd been holding. She quickly slid out of the dress, wishing this evening could've ended on a different note.

She laid the dress out on the bed and stepped back. She eased out of one heel and then the other, and laid those at the foot of the bed near the dress. She pulled out a pair of jean shorts and a tank from her bag and slid into those.

After gathering everything together, she headed out of the master suite and went down to the den. Her heart beat heavy in her chest, nerves curled through her. She had no idea what to expect or what he wanted to tell her. All she knew was she needed some space. She needed to clear her thoughts and really evaluate what she wanted to do with her life.

She'd been thrust into this situation with Sam in such a pressurized manner, and then she'd fallen into a heated fling. Now she needed to take a giant step back and sort out each of her thoughts.

Pulling in a shaky breath, Maty stepped around the corner and into the den. Only the soft glow of an accent lamp on the desk lit the room. Sam stood at the window, staring out into the dark night. Maty took one step into the room, but remained at a good distance.

"The letter is on the desk if you want to read it," he said, without turning to face her.

Maty considered her options, but was intrigued and still stunned by this entire ordeal so she crossed the office, sat her belongings down and picked up the paper.

She scanned the words at first, trying to take in all of it at once, but then she went back through it slowly. The worry and concern came through so clear from the woman who wanted her only son to know the truth and for Sam to help Nick through this difficult time. Maty had never met Nick's mother, but from this letter Maty could tell the woman had been brave.

"I can't imagine what she went through keeping that secret all this time." Maty placed the letter back on the desk. "Are you ever going to tell Rusty?"

Sam glanced over his shoulder, his eyes raked over her and she couldn't suppress the shiver. He looked at her with hunger whether she wore a ten-thousand-dollar gown or a pair of cut-off shorts.

"Probably not," Sam replied. "He deserves nothing from me, certainly not the truth. If he wanted to know about his child, he would've helped my mother instead of buying her off."

Maty glanced around the den, unsure of what to do next. While he battled his demons with Rusty and his mother, Maty wondered where she would have even fallen in the lineup of the chaos in his life. Maybe that's another reason why he hadn't told her. Maybe there was too much going on.

Well, she had enough turmoil in her life as well. She couldn't just give him a pass right now, not when her own emotions were so jumbled up and all over the place.

"Before we left earlier, you said there was something you wanted to tell me."

Maty turned her attention to him. "What?"

Sam started toward her, his eyes fixed on her. "When we were ready to walk out the door for the gala," he reminded her. "You stopped and said you'd talk to me later. Do you remember what you wanted to say?"

She remembered. Nothing had changed, yet everything had.

Her feelings hadn't just vanished. She couldn't turn off the emotions or ignore the pull. She could, however, guard her heart from here on out.

"I was going to tell you that I love you," she replied with a tip of her chin. "I was foolish enough to think maybe we were starting over, that we were a team—I believe that's the word you used."

He took another step and started to reach for her. "Maty—"

"No." She held up her hands and moved back.

"That's what I was thinking and now you know. I need to get out of here. It's late and I'm exhausted."

"Where will you go?" he asked. "Just stay. Stay in another room and I promise not to bother you. Hell, I'll leave. I need to know you're safe."

Maty shook her head. "Don't be absurd. You're not leaving your own house. I'm a big girl, Sam. I'll be fine. I'm not your concern anymore."

Something shifted in his gaze, something that she couldn't quite pinpoint, but she knew Sam enough to know that he battled so much within himself.

Maybe they both needed time to think, to heal.

"You weren't just my concern," he countered. "You were my life. Then, now. I want to see where this goes. I don't deserve to ask for a second chance, but… I'm asking anyway."

Maty wished life was so easy that a few simple words could wash away all the hurt and build a bridge to start new on the other side of pain.

"We rushed into all of this," she told him. "And it was fun. It was great. I actually felt like you might be falling for me."

"I was. I am." He raked a hand over his hair, making it stand on end. "Damn it, Maty. Take the master bedroom. Lock the door. I promise I won't bother you and we can talk in the morning. Just don't leave when you're this upset and it's late. You have nowhere else to go."

He made a valid point. She had nowhere to go and very little money right now.

"I'll take a guest room," she told him. "I can't guarantee anything come morning, but I'm tired and you're right that I have no place else."

That hurt to say, hurt even more to live. She'd never been so vulnerable in all her life, but she still had common sense.

"I'll get your stuff moved," he told her.

"I can get it," she replied. "I just… I need some space."

The muscle in his jaw clenched as he nodded. His dark eyes never wavered from hers. Maty wanted him to wrap those strong arms around her and tell her that everything was fine, that all of this was a big misunderstanding, that Rusty wasn't his father and he hadn't lied.

Since there was nothing left to say for now, Maty turned, grabbed her things and decided to claim the farthest room away from Sam's.

"I love you, too."

The soft words were delivered in such a heartfelt, genuine tone, Maty stilled, but she didn't turn around. She didn't want to look in his eyes right now. Maybe that made her a coward, but she mentally and emotionally couldn't handle it right now.

"I hope you mean that," she murmured, then walked out with her broken heart and unshed tears.

Sixteen

The morning light slid through the sheers over the balcony doors and Maty rolled over to grab her phone. She'd gotten little sleep and was no less confused and hurt this morning than she'd been last night.

Sam had kept his promise and left her alone. She tapped on her screen and saw where he'd texted her.

I'm at the distillery so take all the time and space you need. I meant what I said last night.

He loved her.

Part of her fully believed he did, but the other part, the part that was in pain, wondered how he could keep something so monumental from her if he had such strong feelings.

Maty sat up in bed, but didn't reply. She did notice that he sent that text at about four in the morning, so clearly he hadn't slept well, either. A guilty conscience would do that to a person.

She shoved her hair from her face and opened a social media app. Maybe snooping into other people's lives would help her forget hers for a moment.

The first thing she spotted was a shared link to an interview with Sam about the opening of his distillery. And damn if she didn't click on it to read more about the man she couldn't ignore.

She scrolled through, reading the answers to how he'd gotten his start, how he bought the building for the distillery and turned it into Hawkins. She scrolled on down and saw an image of the two of them. A candid shot with his hand on the small of her back, she was laughing at something someone said off camera, and Sam had his eyes firmly fixed on her. She zoomed in and stared at his face. There was an expression in his eyes that she hadn't seen before…or maybe she'd just never taken the time to really notice.

He looked at her as if she were his whole world. That gala had been bustling with so many important people, billionaires from all over, from all fields, and in the still shot of this moment Sam didn't appear to care about any of that.

Maty's throat clogged with emotion as she continued scrolling. She got to the question about the bottle design and how he came up with that. Beneath the question was a photo of the bottle.

She stared at it, wondering herself how he'd come up with it. The bottle with its square edges, tall and thin base with an etched glass neck and a gold top. A bold *H* dominated the front of the glass bottle.

Maty continued down to read his answer and she gasped.

When I was first dreaming of all of this, someone very special to me drew this bottle. She was just playing around, but it has stuck with me all these years. I knew if I ever reached this point, there was no other design I would want.

She quickly scrolled back to the bottle image again.

Memories came flooding back. She remembered the day she'd doodled this bottle. They had been eating pizza and drinking a beer that he had brewed. It was awful, the pizza and the beer, but they'd laughed and dreamed and she'd scribbled out a design.

And he'd kept it alive all these years.

The cracks and bruises on her heart started to mend. Her vision started to blur as tears formed. She dropped her phone into her lap and finally let the tears flow. They flowed for the loss of her parents, the irreversible paralysis to her brother, the blackmail from Rusty and the betrayal from Sam.

So many blows in such a short time. She had to

heal from the inside out and really evaluate what she wanted for her future. She needed a vision, something to hold on to and give her the hope she'd been missing for so long.

Sam was that hope.

Even when she'd pushed him away last night, he'd opened his heart and revealed his true feelings…and she fully believed he loved her. The look on his face in that picture, the fact that he'd held on to that drawing from sixteen years ago, and how he'd protected her from Rusty and cared for her brother. He continually showed her over and over his true feelings.

He might have made a mistake, but perhaps she had too when she left all those years ago. Maybe she should've believed they could have it all, careers and love.

So why couldn't they have it all now? There was nothing stopping them.

Maty swiped the dampness from her face and tossed the covers aside. She wanted to get to the distillery right now, but first she had to at least shower and not show up looking like a haggard insomniac. She was about to reclaim her future…she had to look her best for the man she loved.

"You okay, man?"

Sam blinked and shook his head as he turned his attention from the empty bourbon bottles to Nick.

"Yeah," Sam lied. "Just didn't get much sleep last night."

A complete understatement. He'd lain awake all night hoping to hear Maty outside his door, praying she'd come to talk to him and give them another chance. He'd screwed up in not telling her the truth about Rusty. He should've known he could trust her, that she had never had a vindictive bone in her body.

"We can do this another day," Nick told him.

Silvia reached out and patted Sam's arm. "It's okay to take some time off."

Sam shook his head. "No. I'd rather work, and there's nothing else I'd rather do than get my brother and his wife all set up with their first order for their resort."

They'd decided yesterday to meet this morning and Sam hadn't wanted to cancel or postpone. No matter what was going on in his personal life, he had a distillery to run and this order was too important for Nick and Silvia.

The clicking of heels pulled his attention toward the lobby. Maty strode through the open area, heading straight toward where they stood gathered around a tasting table. She looked too damn good with her long hair down and wavy, skinny jeans, black heels and a simple black tank. Those glossy red lips hit him with a punch of lust.

He glanced to Silvia and Nick who were both smiling like they knew something he didn't.

"Excuse me," he muttered as he stepped away from the table.

Sam crossed the distance to stand before Maty and she offered a smile that had all the nerves in his belly easing.

"Just to be clear, you were a jerk for not telling me the truth."

Sam bit the inside of his cheek to keep from laughing, but he nodded his agreement. "I was."

"But I can see your side of things and I don't believe you were purposely being sneaky."

This was all so different from their conversation last night. He'd thought for sure the more she thought about what he'd done, the angrier she'd be.

"What made you see my side?" he asked.

She glanced over his shoulder and Sam turned to see their audience smiling like idiots. He laughed.

"Ignore them," he told her.

"We can go," Silvia suggested.

"No, we can't," Nick added. "I want to make sure he doesn't screw this up again."

Sam couldn't help but laugh a second time.

Maty stepped around him and walked to the tasting table. He watched as she picked up one of the empty bottles and held it out.

"This," she explained. "Why didn't you tell me you used my design?"

Sam shoved his hands in his pockets and shifted his stance. While he'd rather not have Nick and Silvia watching everything, he also wasn't letting this moment go. Maty had come to him and he had to believe that meant she wanted to give him another chance.

"I wanted to surprise you last night when I revealed it to everyone," he explained. "I wasn't sure if you'd remember, but I just thought the gala was the perfect place to show you I used your design… and to tell you that I love you."

"We really should leave them alone," Silvia whispered.

Nick took her hand. "We'll be right over there," he said, pointing toward the lobby.

Sam waited until they walked away and turned back to Maty. "I do love you," he reiterated because he couldn't tell her enough. "I wanted last night to be perfect and special for both of us. I want you on this journey with me because you've been there from the beginning."

Maty's eyes welled with tears as she bit her bottom lip. Sam couldn't take this distance for another minute. He reached for her at the same time she reached for him. He grabbed hold of her hands and pulled them to his chest.

"Tell me that we can try this again," he implored. "Tell me that I didn't screw up to the point you want nothing to do with me."

Maty leaned forward and touched her forehead to his chest. "I want everything to do with you. Everything," she murmured. "I know why you did what you did and I know you love me. I'm just scared, Sam. Scared of a future with my career, my brother, you."

He eased back and tipped her chin up so he could see her eyes. "You're the strongest woman I know. You have nothing to be scared of on your own, but with me at your side, we'll slay everything in our path."

"You sound so certain that everything will work out."

A tear slipped down her cheek and he swiped it away with the pad of his thumb. He never wanted to see her cry, never wanted her to feel any pain.

"I am."

"What about Rusty?" she asked. "He'll try to destroy both of us."

Sam smiled and framed her face. "Listen to me—Lockwood is a nonissue. He's not a problem for me and he sure as hell won't be a problem for you. Nick told me this morning that Rusty was arrested last night for his connection to stealing from Milestones. I'm sure he'll be out soon thanks to his other lawyers and he'll fight the charges as best he can, but he's too busy now to be a problem for us."

Maty closed her eyes and pulled in a shaky breath. Sam took the opportunity to feather his lips across hers and a relief swept through him when she wrapped her arms around his neck and opened to him.

Sam settled his hands on her waist and held her close, never wanting to let her go. She threaded her fingers through his hair and eased back just enough to look up at him.

"I guess this means I'm staying in Green Valley," she said with a smile.

"Forever," he told her.

"Excuse me."

Sliding his arm around her waist, Sam turned to the lobby. Nick and Silvia were staring at a stranger who had just come in. The man was tall, with wide shoulders, jet-black hair. He screamed money in a groomed and polished sort of way.

"I'm sorry to just drop in," the man stated. "I know you're not open to the public today, but I was hoping I would catch someone. I'm looking for Sam Hawkins or Nick Campbell."

Nick's gaze jerked over to Sam. Maty tensed at Sam's side.

He curled his fingers around her hip, offering silent assurance. "I'm Sam Hawkins."

"And I'm Nick. What's this about?"

But Sam knew. He looked in the man's eyes and knew before the words came out of his mouth.

"My name is Reese Conrad and I know this is going to sound crazy," the man said as he pulled a piece of paper from his back pocket. "But I got this letter in the mail."

Maty gasped and Sam released her as he took a

step forward toward Nick. Nick's eyes remained on the stranger and the letter…no doubt the one from his mother.

"I think you two are my brothers."

They'd finally found the third sibling. A total stranger, but Sam had heard the name Reese Conrad. He was part of the Conrad family who owned elite, upscale restaurants all along the East Coast.

But who was this stranger, really? Reading about someone, seeing their name and face in a magazine or online didn't give much insight into their integrity. Only the positives were highlighted. So how would Reese Conrad change the course of events with Rusty?

Sam felt Maty's delicate hand on his back and he knew no matter what came in this next chapter, he could do anything with her at his side.

Whoever this stranger and half brother was, he would certainly change the dynamics of the relationship with everyone involved. Maty hoped for Sam and Nick's sake, that Reese was nothing like their monstrous father.

* * * *

Don't miss Reese's story
Scandalous Engagement
Available June 2020!

**WE HOPE YOU ENJOYED
THIS BOOK FROM**

**H HARLEQUIN
DESIRE**

*Luxury, scandal, desire—welcome to
the lives of the American elite.*

Be transported to the worlds of oil barons, family dynasties,
moguls and celebrities. Get ready for juicy plot twists,
delicious sensuality and intriguing scandal.

6 NEW BOOKS AVAILABLE EVERY MONTH!

SPECIAL EXCERPT FROM

⊕ HARLEQUIN

DESIRE

*To protect her from a relentless ex, restaurateur Reese
Conrad proposes to his best friend, Josie Coleman.
But their fake engagement reveals real feelings, and
Josie sees Reese in a whole new way. And just as things
heat up, a shocking revelation changes everything!*

Read on for a sneak peek at
Scandalous Engagement
by USA TODAY *bestselling author Jules Bennett.*

"What's that smile for?" he asked.

She circled the island and placed a hand over his heart. "You're
just remarkable. I mean, I've always known, but lately you're just
proving yourself more and more."

He released the wine bottle and covered her hand with his...and
that's when she remembered the kiss. She shouldn't have touched
him—she should've kept her distance because there was that look
in his eyes again. Where had this come from? When did he start
looking at her like he wanted to rip her clothes off and have his
naughty way with her?

"We need to talk about it," he murmured.

It. As if saying the word *kiss* would somehow make this situation
weirder. And as if she hadn't thought of anything else since *it* had
happened.

"Nothing to talk about," she told him, trying to ignore the warmth
and strength between his hand and his chest.

"You can't say you weren't affected."

"I didn't say that."

He tipped his head, somehow making that penetrating stare even
more potent. "It felt like more than a friend kiss."

Way to state the obvious.

"And more than just a practice," he added.

Josie's heart kicked up. They were too close, talking about things that were too intimate. No matter what she felt, what she thought she wanted, this wasn't right. She couldn't ache for her best friend in such a physical way. If that kiss changed things, she couldn't imagine how anything more would affect this relationship.

"We can't go there again," she told him. "I mean, you're a good kisser—"

"Good? That kiss was a hell of a lot better than just good."

She smiled. "Fine. It was pretty incredible. Still, we can't get caught up in this whole fake-engagement thing and lose sight of who we really are."

His free hand came up and brushed her hair away from her face. "I haven't lost sight of anything. And I'm well aware of who we are…and what I want."

Why did that sound so menacing in the most delicious of ways? Why was her body tingling so much from such simple touches when she'd firmly told herself to not get carried away?

Wait. Was he leaning in closer?

"Reese, what are you doing?" she whispered.

"Testing a theory."

His mouth grazed hers like a feather. Her knees literally weakened as she leaned against him for support. Reese continued to hold her hand against his chest, but he wrapped the other arm around her waist, urging her closer.

There was no denying the sizzle or spark or whatever the hell was vibrating between them. She'd always thought those cheesy expressions were so silly, but there was no perfect way to describe such an experience.

And kissing her best friend was quite an experience…

Don't miss what happens next in…
Scandalous Engagement
by USA TODAY bestselling author Jules Bennett.

Available June 2020 wherever
Harlequin Desire books and ebooks are sold.

Harlequin.com

IF YOU ENJOYED THIS BOOK
WE THINK YOU WILL ALSO LOVE

Escape to exotic locations where passion knows no bounds.

Welcome to the glamorous lives of royals and billionaires, where passion knows no bounds. Be swept into a world of luxury, wealth and exotic locations.

8 NEW BOOKS AVAILABLE EVERY MONTH!

Love Harlequin romance?

DISCOVER.

Be the first to find out about promotions, news and exclusive content!

[f] Facebook.com/HarlequinBooks

[𝕏] Twitter.com/HarlequinBooks

[◎] Instagram.com/HarlequinBooks

[𝕡] Pinterest.com/HarlequinBooks

ReaderService.com

EXPLORE.

Sign up for the Harlequin e-newsletter and download a free book from any series at
TryHarlequin.com

CONNECT.

Join our Harlequin community to share your thoughts and connect with other romance readers!
Facebook.com/groups/HarlequinConnection

HARLEQUIN

Heartfelt or suspenseful, inspiring or passionate, Harlequin has your happily-ever-after.

With new books published every month, you are sure to find the satisfying escape you know you deserve.